TO HAVE HER AGAIN

KAY SHANEE

B. Love Publications

ABOUT THE AUTHOR

Kay is a forty-something wife and mother, born and raised in the Midwest. During the day, she is a high school teacher and track coach. In her free time, she enjoys spending time with her family and friends. Her favorite pastime is reading and writing romance novels about the DOPENESS of BLACK LOVE.

SYNOPSIS

Myles Abbott was a hustler by nature. His reputation as an astute dealer superseded him. However, he'd give it all up to have and to hold the woman his heart belonged to. If only he didn't hesitate. Reluctantly accepting her departure, he dove deeper into the same street life he was ready to leave behind. Putting up a wall around his heart, he determined love would never get him again.

Everleigh Noble was torn apart when she was forced to decide the safety of her family would triumph over her lover's heart. Over time, burying the agony of her choice, she finds a way to prosper. She almost has it all; a dream career and a rich, handsome fiancé. Still, something's not right. Below the surface is where her true heart beats.

Years later, tragedy strikes, bringing Myles and Everleigh together. The past refuses to be left behind. Yet, when secrets are revealed, and old wounds resurface, some things will live while others will need to die. Will their love be amongst what survives?

WARNING!

This book contains some topics that may be sensitive for some. If miscarriages, abortions, stillborn births, or infertility trigger you, you may want to refrain from reading this book. Please feel free to choose another book from my catalog.

PROLOGUE

Myles had been in the streets all night, which wasn't his intention. Some shit went down at the warehouse that had to be taken care of right away. Everleigh had been blowing up his phone all night. Although he did send her a text, letting her know that he would be home as soon as he could, she continued to call him. He mentally prepared himself for her to go off on him the moment he walked into their apartment.

After parking his truck in the private parking garage that was attached to their high rise apartment building, he got on the elevator and took it to the twenty-fourth floor. Once the elevator stopped on his floor, he stepped off, and with every step that he took towards their apartment, he became more and more nervous. Myles had squared up with people that outweighed him by a hundred pounds and came out victorious. He'd even been responsible for people taking their last breath. Yet, here he was, nervous about the confrontation that he knew awaited him inside the apartment.

When he made it to the door of the apartment that he'd shared with Everleigh for the past two years, he entered the code on the keypad, and slowly opened the door. After closing it softly behind him and entering the same code to lock the door, he looked around.

The sun had already risen, and with the open floor plan, he could see the living room, dining room, and kitchen. As his eyes scanned the area, he didn't see anything out of place.

In the kitchen, he put his keys on the counter and grabbed a bottle of water from the fridge. After downing it in a few gulps, he tossed the bottle in the recycle bin and headed to the bedroom. When he walked into the room, he wasn't expecting Everleigh to be sitting at the foot of the bed, with two large suitcases on either side of her.

"Whatchu doin'? Wassup with the luggage?" he asked.

Everleigh was fed up. Since about a year into their relationship that started four years ago, she had been pushing him to leave the streets. She was only eighteen at the time they started dating, and Myles was twenty-two. As much as she loved him, she knew that wasn't the kind of life she wanted to live. He made a bunch of promises that she felt he had no intention of keeping.

"I'm leaving," she replied.

"Leavin'? To go where?"

"I'm moving to L.A."

Myles couldn't believe his ears, but he knew Everleigh wouldn't play with him like that.

"Baby—" he began before she interrupted him.

"Myles, don't," she told him calmly. "Don't stand there and lie to me like you've been doing for the past three years. I'm tired of being alone all the time, and I'm tired of worrying if you'll make it home. This shit is stressful, and I can't do it anymore."

"Damn, Leigh! You act like you ain't know what the fuck I was about when we hooked up. Why is it a problem now?"

She stood from the bed and approached him. "Don't yell at me. Talk to me the way I'm talking to you," she demanded.

"My bad, baby. I just don't understand why—"

"It's always been a problem. You know I was never comfortable with this, but you made me fall in love with your ass. I thought maybe you loved me enough to change."

"I love you more than anything in this world. I'm tryin' to leave this shit alone. It's not as easy as you think."

"Yes, it is. Stop hustling and get a real job. I don't want to lose you to the damn streets, Myles, and that's what will happen if you don't stop."

"What the fuck kinda job I'm gon' find with only a high school diploma that will pay for us to live like this?" He lifted his hand and waved it around the room.

"Who says we have to live like this? *You* wanted this, not me. You know I don't give a damn about material things. I want *you*." She poked him in the chest. "I want you home with me every night. I want you safe and out of harm's way. I want us to grow old together, and I know..." She began to cry, and Myles pulled her into his arms, hugging her tight.

"Baby, please. Just give me a lil more time. You promised not to give up on me."

She pushed away. "I can't, Myles. I love you, but I can't. I accepted a job, and it's a great opportunity. I already told my parents. I have to go before I miss my flight."

"You accepted a job? You been plannin' this?"

Myles was stunned. He knew that Everleigh would be upset about him coming home after the sun had risen, for the second night in a row, and he expected them to have a few words about it. Her leaving had never crossed his mind, and the fact that she'd been planning to leave, for some time it seems, didn't sit well with him.

"I knew you wouldn't consider my feelings. I—"

"You didn't know shit! I coulda walked my ass in here and told you I was done hustlin', and you still woulda been prepared to walk out that door. L.A., Leigh? You found and took a job in Los Angeles? How we supposed to do this shit?" He pointed to her and then himself.

Her eyes met the floor, and he slid his index finger under her chin to lift her head. The pool of water in her eyes did nothing to calm the storm the was brewing inside him.

"How long you been plannin' to leave me?"

"I—"

"How long, Leigh?"

"Three months," she whispered.

"You been plottin' and plannin' for three months?" He took a step back as he nodded his head in disbelief. "You had one fuckin' foot out the door for three whole months?"

"You wouldn't listen. I tried to—"

"You know what, Leigh, no need to explain. I wish you the best."

The coldness in his voice sent chills down Everleigh's spine. The darkness in his eyes made her have second thoughts about her decision. He walked past her and into the bathroom, closing the door behind him.

That was the last time they saw each other.

CHAPTER 1

I t was an abnormally warm day for Seattle at the beginning of June, and surprisingly, not raining. Myles had been detailing a car for the past four hours and was glad to be almost done. The customer would be there in about thirty minutes to pick it up, and then he would be done for the day.

When he decided that it was time for him to make some changes in his life, Myles didn't know what he would do. He'd been in the streets for twenty years, and in that time, he managed to put away a lot of cash, invested in a few stocks, and the last couple years, he earned an associate's degree in business. But mostly, all he knew how to do was move weight.

Right around the time he started contemplating doing something different with his life, Myles was at his mom's house, detailing her car. One of his boys from back in the day was driving by, and he stopped to catch up. He'd recently been released from prison, and they hadn't spoken in years. Joe commented on how good the car looked and asked him how much he charged.

It was then that a lightbulb went off in Myles's head, and he rolled with the idea, researching what he would need to do to start a legitimate auto detailing business. The process wasn't complicated, and he slowly began transitioning from street nigga to a legitimate businessman. Once he filed the paperwork to form an LLC, he continued to work out of his mom's garage for several months, establishing a paper trail for his business.

Soon after that, he sold his condo, using half the money to pay off his mom's house, then moved back in with his mom for a few months. Not long after, he took over the lease for his sister's townhome when she moved to Chicago. Transitioning from the lifestyle that he'd been living for the past twenty years, to an upstanding citizen wasn't as easy as they made it look in books and movies. The government and the IRS were a real thing, so he had to be smart.

The building that now housed his car detailing shop was rundown when he bought it about seven months ago from an older Black man. He just wanted to get rid of it, which made buying it with cash a lot easier. Myles had a lot of repairs done, along with getting the outside painted. It wasn't anything special, but the perfect way for him to transition into his new life.

Just as he finished the car, he heard the bell that he had installed on the door in the front part of the garage. Myles Abbott Auto Detailing, or MAAD, currently only had one employee, which was him, so he had to see who was at the front door.

When he saw who was waiting for him, his dick stiffened. Nyema Bates was a woman that Myles had been dealing with on a sexual level for quite some time, probably close to four years. She wasn't his girlfriend, although, in her mind, she considered herself his. Nyema was in love with Myles, there was no doubt about that, and prayed every night that he would fall in love with her. What she didn't know was that his heart belonged to someone else, it had for all of his adult life, and he had no intention of changing that.

Myles liked Nyema, but that's where it ended. She was a gorgeous, brown-skinned beauty that many would call slim-thick because of her ample ass and small waist. Her hair was natural, but most of the time, she wore braids. The one thing that he didn't like was that she wore too much makeup, along with those fake eyelashes that women seemed to think were attractive. Myles thought all that extra was unnecessary, especially for Nyema, because she was naturally beautiful.

"Wassup?" he said, licking his lips as he adjusted his dick.

Nyema was wearing a pair of biker shorts, a black T-shirt, and some Nikes. Myles's eyes roamed her body, and if he had some condoms on him, he'd take her to the bathroom and bend her over the sink. The main reason he kept Nyema around was because her sex game was top notch. The pussy was magnificent, and she could suck a dick like a champ.

Although the physical connection between the two of them was great, Myles didn't feel anything else for her. He cared about her in the sense that he didn't want anything bad to happen to her, but he had no desire to be in a relationship with her. Aside from Nyema, he fucked with a few other women when she got too clingy.

"Nothing. I thought you might be close to finishing up for the day, so I stopped by."

"Cool. The customer should be here any minute to pick up her car."

"Cool. You mind if I wait?"

He shrugged his shoulders. "Ain't nowhere for you to sit in here. You mind waitin' in your car?"

"Okay."

She leaned in and tried to kiss him, which Myles thought was odd because she knew he didn't do that. The most she'd ever gotten from him was a kiss on the cheek or forehead. He quickly turned his head so that her lips landed on his cheek. Nyema was disappointed that her attempt to feel his lips on hers had failed. She went to her car, and Myles went back to the garage area and put away all his supplies. As he finished, a car pulled up, and the owner of the one he'd just detailed got out of the backseat. She entered the front part of the garage as Myles entered the same area through another door.

"You're right on time. I just finished," Myles greeted.

"Great! I hope it wasn't too bad. My kids have no respect for my car. Sometimes I look in that back seat and want to scream," she said.

"Not at all, Ms. Frank. I've seen a lot worse."

Using his iPad, he rang her up, and she followed the instructions on the screen to complete her payment.

"Just step right out front, and I'll pull your car out of the garage for you to take a look."

"Okay, thank you."

Once he pulled out, he stepped out of the car and allowed her to do an inspection. She was pleased and offered him an additional tip, which he declined, reminding her that she'd already paid a fifteen percent gratuity. Myles had that automatically added to every transaction because he knew some customers were cheap as hell. He didn't have a problem accepting an extra tip from men, but he could never bring himself to do so with women.

After Ms. Frank pulled off, he went back inside to grab his phone and the keys, before turning on the alarm and locking up the place. Nyema was leaning against the driver's side door of her car when he walked back out. He smiled as he approached her because he knew that soon, his dick would be stretching her pussy nice and wide.

"Why are you smiling?" she asked.

"I can't smile?"

"I mean, yeah. I was just wondering."

"No reason. Just glad to be done for the day. Whatchu 'bout to get into?"

"Nothing. I was gonna ask you that."

He stood directly in front of her, sandwiching her body between him and her car.

"I was hopin' I could get into you," he said, kissing her cheek.

She smiled and put her arms around his neck. "I think that can be arranged. Kai is with her dad for a couple days. My place or yours?"

"I gotta go take a shower, anyway, so you can meet me at my crib."

He dug in his pocket and took out a wad of cash, pulling off a hundred dollar bill.

"Stop by that lil Mexican spot and get us somethin' to eat, I'm starvin'. Keep the change." He added a wink.

They parted ways, and as Nyema drove to the Mexican restaurant, she couldn't stop smiling. Lately, Myles had been treating her more like his girlfriend and not just a fuck buddy. A few months ago, he finally let her come to his place, and after four years, Nyema thought that was a *huge* step in the right direction.

She pulled up to his townhouse about thirty minutes later. Myles answered the door shirtless, in a pair of basketball shorts. Her pussy throbbed when her eyes landed on his dick print. Myles was definitely blessed in that department, and it was part of the reason Nyema had stuck around so long, with no real commitment from him. Not even Kai's father could bless her pussy the way Myles did. At one point, she couldn't imagine anyone being better than him, but he was no comparison to Myles.

He took the bag of food from her hand and placed it on a table that was next to the door. Roughly, he pulled her further inside, then closed and locked the door behind her.

"Get out them shorts," he demanded.

Without a moment of hesitation, Nyema toed off her shoes and pushed her shorts down, taking her underwear with them. Myles walked her to the back of the couch, and she placed her hands on the back of it. Behind her, she heard him opening a condom, and seconds later, he slid into her wet folds.

"Mmm, shit," she moaned.

He gave her a few seconds to adjust to his size before he slowly pulled out and plunged even deeper inside.

"Oh, damn, Myles!"

One of his hands held her by the waist, the other pressed on her back, pushing her deeper into the couch. It had been several days since the last time Myles had busted a nut, and Nyema's pussy felt amazing. But he wasn't the type of lover that gave verbal praise, so she would never know how good she felt gripping his dick.

He stroked her long, slow, and deep, bringing her to the brink of an orgasm. Nyema reached between her legs to give herself that extra boost she needed. Usually, that would piss Myles off, and she knew that. Today, he went ahead and let her be great. All he wanted to do was dump this load into this condom, eat, and go to bed.

"Oh, Myles, baby. I'm cummin'," Nyema sang.

Her pussy clutched around him as she reached her peak, and just as he was about to bust, he pulled out and jacked himself to completion. Nyema hated that he did that but never said anything to him about it. Even with protection, Myles was paranoid about planting his seeds inside of a woman with whom he didn't want a future. He didn't care how they felt about it. Almost an hour later, Myles was walking Nyema to the door.

"It's still early," she whined.

"I know."

"Why are you making me leave already?" She looked sexy with her pouty lips, but not sexy enough for Myles to change his plans.

"I got an early morning, and I'm 'bout to go to bed."

"I told you, Kai is with her dad."

Myles was comfortable enough with Nyema to let her know where he lived, but staying overnight was a whole different ball game. He knew that if she stayed overnight, she would think more about the status of their relationship, and he couldn't have that.

"Naw, I'm good. I'll catch up with you in a few days."

He kissed her forehead and ushered her out the door. Before closing it, he made sure she was securely inside her car and backing out of the driveway. Her attempts to make their relationship more than what it was, didn't go unnoticed. The more she pressed, the more he considered ending it altogether.

CHAPTER 2

The following day, Myles had a limousine to detail. It took him about six hours, but when he was finished, it looked brand new. Not long after the car was picked up, the owner of the limousine company called Myles to inquire about contracting him to detail all of their vehicles. After discussing the details for the meeting, Myles went home and showered, then decided to stop by the Noble residence.

Mr. and Mrs. Noble were like family to him. Even though it had been years since he dated their daughter, he visited them regularly and made sure they were never in need. Ms. Dinah doted on him a great deal. If he couldn't get a home-cooked meal from his mother, he knew Ms. Dinah would hook him up.

Mr. Everette took him under his wing. The last time Myles saw his father, he was a child, so he appreciated the things he learned from him.

"Hey, son," he greeted Myles when he opened the door. "You refuse to use the key we gave you, huh."

They hugged before Myles replied with, "It's for emergencies, and I hope I never have to use it."

"That's not the only reason we gave you a key but, I won't keep pressing the issue. You must have known Dinah was cooking today."

"No, I didn't, but I was hopin'. What's on the menu?"

"Hell, I don't know, but it sure smells good. It don't much matter because I'm gon' eat whatever she puts in front of me."

The Nobles were already in their seventies. Their daughter, Everleigh, was an only child, and they had a hard time conceiving her, not being successful until they were in their forties. They'd always been accepting of Myles, and even after the break-up, they continued to welcome him into their home.

"I'm with that, Mr. Everette. I haven't had a meal yet that she's cooked that hasn't been delicious."

"Well, come on in, and let's sit down. The game is still on."

Myles followed him into the family room. There was a baseball game playing on the television. Although Myles wasn't a big fan of the game, he kept up with the Mariners just to have something to talk about with Mr. Everette during the summer months. As he was about to sit down on the couch, Ms. Dinah walked in. Myles greeted her with a hug and a kiss on the cheek before being seated.

"You must be busy these days. We haven't seen you in a few weeks," Ms. Dinah said.

"I'm sorry, Ms. Dinah. Since I opened the shop, I've been busy and tired. Right now, it's only me, but business has been great. I may have to hire a few people."

"That's wonderful, son. You know, we're proud of you."

"Thank you. I know, over the years, I ain't made the best choices. I'm tryin' to fix that, though," Myles humbly replied.

He never discussed how he made his money with the Nobles, but they knew he was in the streets. Instead of pressuring him about it, Ms. Dinah always let him know that she prayed for him and encouraged him to do things in the community. He and Mr. Everette spent a lot of time talking, and he stayed dropping gems on Myles. Two of the most important things he learned from him was how to treat his future wife and how to invest his money.

"Everyone makes choices that they aren't proud of. It's called life. You've made some pretty good ones, too. The time and money you invest with the kids at the Boys and Girls club is something you should be proud of. Your soul and spirit have always been genuine. That means a lot these days," Ms. Dinah continued complimenting him.

"I appreciate that, Ms. Dinah. You both have definitely had a positive impact on me. Years ago, you could have sent me on my way, but instead, you helped me become a man. I know it took a little while for it all to sink in, but I'm grateful to know you."

Myles stood and hugged Ms. Dinah again. Her husband was focused on the baseball game, but heard the exchange between them.

"Y'all too damn sentimental for me today. I'm trying to watch the game," he fussed.

Myles laughed as he sat back down. Ms. Dinah was always like that with him. She truly thought of him as a son; they both did.

"Oh hush, old man. Dinner's done, anyway."

She turned to leave the family room, and Myles followed, heading to the bathroom to wash his hands. Soon after, the three of them were sitting at the dining room table. Ms. Dinah made cabbage, cornbread, macaroni and cheese, and ham. It wasn't often that Myles had a chance to eat like that, but he thoroughly enjoyed it when he did.

"Is your mom still enjoying living in Chicago, now that she's survived a winter?" Ms. Dinah asked.

He laughed as he thought about how much she complained during the winter months. "She said that winter was brutal, but she's happy. She loves seeing her grandkids all the time."

"I'm sure she does. It doesn't look like we'll be getting any grand-children anytime soon, from you or Ev."

Although he could detect a hint of sadness in her voice, he was happy to know that Everleigh hadn't given birth to another man's baby.

"I can only speak for myself, but children aren't anywhere in my near future. I haven't been able to find the right woman."

"If Everleigh would come to her senses and leave that asshole she's with—"

"Everette!" Ms. Dinah exclaimed.

"What?" he replied innocently. "You know Easton is as big an asshole as they come. I don't know what she sees in him."

It was not a secret that he was not very fond of his daughter's fiancé. He'd shared his dislike with Myles, and whoever else would listen, many times before.

"We don't have to see it, as long as she does."

"Obviously, she don't see too well."

Myles watched them go back and forth, and for a moment, imagined it being him and Everleigh, forty years from then. He shook off the thoughts because the odds of that happening were very slim. The last time he laid eyes on Everleigh was twelve years ago.

"Regardless of how we feel about Easton, she needs to feel like we support her. I think Ev knows that he's not the man for her." She paused momentarily, eating a few bites of food before continuing. "I mean, he proposed two years ago, and they haven't mentioned a thing about getting married. That doesn't even make sense."

"You wouldn't stand for that, would you, Myles?" he asked.

"Umm, stand for...?"

"If you asked Ev to marry you, would you wait years to get married?"

He shook his head. "No, sir. Honestly, at this point, I'd take her ass—my bad, I'd take her to the courthouse, and we'd be married within a week."

"See, that's what I'm talking about. Easton is as weak as they come. He probably don't wanna marry Ev no more than she wants to marry him. They're just wasting time," Mr. Everett said.

Somehow, the trio managed to talk about Everleigh at some point during each of Myles's visits. Generally, Myles kept quiet when Everleigh was the topic. It was bad enough that thoughts of her still invaded his mind after twelve years, talking about her made him miss her even more.

Everleigh had only brought her fiancé to Seattle a few times, so in his defense, the Nobles hadn't had a chance to get to know him. Adding to the fact that Mr. Everette didn't like him, when Easton didn't ask him for Everleigh's hand in marriage, it only increased his disdain for him. The three of them continued to converse throughout dinner. Myles was glad when Ms. Dinah changed the topic and asked him for an update on the volunteering he'd been doing.

For the past eight years or so, Myles had been volunteering at the Boys and Girls Club. He hoped that he could encourage young people to do things differently than he had. Along with financial donations to the organization, volunteering was how Myles gave back to the community that he knew he was partially to blame for ruining. It wasn't enough, and he understood that he had a long way to go to balance out his wrongdoings.

Once dinner was over, Myles offered to clean up when Ms. Dinah expressed that she had a headache and had suddenly become very tired. While Mr. Everette went back to the family room, and Ms. Dinah went to lie down, Myles returned the kitchen to its original condition as best he could. By the time he finished, he'd been there for about three hours. In the family room, Mr. Everette had found another baseball game. As Myles was about to bid his farewell, he asked him to have a seat.

"Can I ask you something, and you give me an honest answer?" he asked.

"Of course."

"Are you still in love with my daughter?" he asked.

The question took Myles by surprise, although he wasn't shocked that Mr. Everette asked him. He'd always been very straightforward.

"I am."

"Why'd you let her leave the way she did? How come you didn't go after her?"

Myles shook his head. "Lettin' her leave is probably my biggest regret in life. The only thing I can say is that I was young, dumb, and stubborn as hell. My pride got in the way, and by the time I thought about goin' after her, I didn't want to disrupt her new life."

"Well, you're older, smarter, and hopefully less stubborn and prideful. Why not now?"

"It's been a long time since I've seen or talked to Leigh. She has a whole life in L.A., with her dream career as a celebrity photographer, and apparently, in love with another nigga. I don't wanna interfere with her happiness."

"What makes you think she's happy?"

"Even though we ain't together, I hope she is."

"Well, I can tell you right now, she's not. For the life of me, I can't understand why she's settling for that uppity nigga."

Mr. Everette looked around to see if his wife was somewhere eavesdropping. She didn't like it when he got on his soapbox and talked negatively about their future son-in-law. She would much prefer Everleigh be with Myles, as well, but she didn't want their dislike for Easton to cause a rift between them.

"She should be home later this month. Let's put a plan in motion for you to get her back."

"A plan?"

"Yes, nigga, a plan. Somehow, you two have managed to not run into each other when she comes to visit. Well, we're about to fix that."

Myles couldn't help but laugh at him. Mr. Everette was a trip, but he appreciated that he'd had his back all these years. For the next thirty minutes or so, they—well, Mr. Everette, told Myles what he needed to do to get Everleigh back. Myles didn't say much. Instead, he nodded in agreement.

Mr. Everette seemed to think that if Myles and Everleigh were in the same room together, sparks would fly, and they would naturally reconnect. Myles had doubts that Everleigh still had feelings for him, after so much time had passed, but felt her father's plan was worth a shot. He was at a place in his life where he would do anything to have Everleigh again, and if that happened, there would be no letting go.

After spending more time there than he'd planned, he finally got up to leave. As Mr. Everette walked Myles to the door, they heard a loud thump come from the bedroom. They took off in that direction, and Myles entered the room first. His heart damn near stopped when he saw Ms. Dinah on the floor, appearing to be unconscious.

CHAPTER 3

E verleigh despised going to any of Easton's corporate events, but that's exactly where she was. He knew she hated attending but insisted that it wouldn't look right if she didn't. Easton was all about appearances, and it drove her absolutely crazy.

While he mingled with his constituents, she was right next to him. One of her arms was looped through his, and in the other hand was a glass of champagne. She thought the drink was disgusting, but she smiled anyway, only speaking at appropriate times. Every so often, she would get lost in her thoughts, and that annoyed the hell out of Easton.

As his fiancée, he expected her to be able to discuss all things related to his role as a corporate real estate executive at Briggs' Real Estate, which was a Fortune 500 company that his family owned.

"He's talking to you," Easton leaned down and whispered in her ear.

"My apologies, Lawrence. I have a huge photo shoot with one of my celebrity clients in the morning. I was going through my mental checklist to ensure I had everything ready to go. It's an early shoot."

"I understand, Everleigh. You're a busy woman. I'm amazed at how you're always by his side at these stuffy events." His eyes roamed her body, taking in her shapely frame that was wrapped in a fitted, black, formal gown. "My wife doesn't even work and can't seem to find the time to come."

"Everleigh makes me a priority. Isn't that right, baby?" Easton said, before leaning down and kissing her temple.

"Mmmhmm," Everleigh replied, rolling her eyes. "Baby, I'm gonna go to the ladies' room. I'll be right back."

As she started to walk away, Easton stopped her and planted a kiss on her lips, then tapped her ass as she walked away. He saw the way Lawrence Black was eyeing his fiancée and wanted to remind him that she was off-limits. Lawrence was known to try to screw any woman that would let him, whether she was taken or not. He had no respect for relationships, including his own. Everleigh knew what Easton was doing. He was usually not a fan of public displays of affection, and she knew that all that extra was his attempt to mark his territory. On her way to the bathroom, she ran into Mrs. Briggs, Easton's mother.

"Sweetheart, why do you keep letting him drag you to these events? I can see the boredom on your face."

Mrs. Shelby Briggs was an amazing woman, and she and Everleigh got along exceptionally well. When her husband passed away from prostate cancer several years ago, before Everleigh had met Easton, she stepped right in and took over the running of his company. Since she'd been at the reigns, business has improved a great deal. From what Everleigh heard, Easton's father, Preston, was a bit of a tyrant and ran his company with an iron fist. He was not well-liked by his employees or business partners. Mrs. Briggs ran the company in a completely different way, and apparently, it was well-received.

"I know, Mrs. Briggs. I keep telling myself this is the last event I'm attending unless it's something major. But Easton can be very convincing, and he lays the guilt trip on pretty heavy."

She shook her head and let her eyes roll. "My son is a spoiled brat. I really should have had more children. I warned you about him and apologized for my contribution to his entitled attitude when we first met. You don't need to attend these stuffy events. Hell, I hate coming to them myself," she whispered that last part as she leaned in to ensure that only I could hear her.

"I know. I'll be sure to sit the next few out. Let me go use the bathroom before my bladder explodes."

"Oh? Does that mean what I think it means?"

Mrs. Briggs, much like Everleigh's parents, were anxious for grandchildren. Although her parents would have preferred she wait until she and Easton married before having children, Mrs. Briggs didn't care when it happened.

"No, ma'am, it definitely is not. I'll connect with you before the end of the night."

Everleigh exited stage left as quickly as she could. Getting into a conversation about her uterus with Easton's mother was the last thing she wanted to do. As Everleigh finished using the bathroom, her phone began to vibrate. She quickly washed and dried her hands before answering.

"Hey, Daddy!" she answered after seeing his name on the display.

"Ev, baby girl, you need to get home."

She could detect that there was something wrong in her father's voice.

"Why? What happened?"

"Your mom...she passed out, and I had to call the ambulance. I don't know what's wrong, but I need you here."

"Oh, God. Okay, Daddy. I'll get there as soon as I can. What hospital?"

"UW Medical Center."

"Okay!"

Ending the call, she let her head rest against the door and closed her eyes, holding her phone against her chest. Tears fell from her eyes as she said a quick prayer for her mother.

"Dear God, please let her be okay."

She went back to the main room and spotted Easton on the other side. The moment he saw her, he knew something was wrong.

"I have to go," Everleigh told him before he could ask her anything.

"Go? Why?"

"My mother—something happened to my mother. My dad had to call the ambulance. I gotta go."

"Oh, baby, I'm sorry. Let's not think the worse. She's gonna be fine," Easton reassured her, then pulled her into a hug. "I'll make sure the company jet is ready when you are. Do you need me to do anything else before you leave?"

Everleigh took a step back and looked up at him. "You aren't coming?" she asked.

"Oh, I wish I could, baby, but I have some important meetings the next few days that I can't miss. If it's serious, I can fly out as soon as they're over."

She was in a state of disbelief as she nodded in his direction. Without saying another word, she turned and walked the other way. Easton was right behind her.

"Ev, don't be upset. These two deals are huge. You know I'd come with you if they weren't."

"It's fine, Easton. Go to your meetings."

By this time, they had made it to the main doors. When they got outside, Everleigh flagged down a cab, and thankfully, one pulled up right away.

"You're taking a cab? Let me get our driver. He should be nearby," he offered.

She had nothing else to say to Easton. He held onto the door, hoping she'd change her mind about the cab. When she didn't respond or move, he dipped his head inside.

"I'll come as soon as my meetings are over," he repeated, deciding not to argue with her about transportation. "Javi will be waiting to take you to the jet."

Everleigh didn't even look in his direction. She told the cab driver where she needed to go and ignored Easton until he closed the door. Right now, all she cared about was getting to her mother.

It didn't take her long to pack a large suitcase and grab her camera bag. She also reached out to another photographer to cover the photo shoot she had the next morning. An hour and a half later, she was on the Briggs' Real Estate company jet, headed to Seattle, praying that whatever was wrong with her mother, it was nothing serious.

CHAPTER 4

Myles followed the ambulance to the hospital. By the time he parked and went inside, they'd already taken Ms. Dinah to the back. Mr. Everette was pacing back and forth in the waiting room of the emergency room. Myles put a hand on his shoulder, and he stilled, before turning around. When he saw Myles, he broke down. Myles put an arm around his shoulders and led him to some chairs in the corner.

"I can't lose her, son. She's my everything," Mr. Everette cried.

In all his thirty-seven years, Myles had never been so touched by the emotions of someone else. It was difficult to see him in so much pain. The Nobles had been together since they were in their twenties. Myles could only imagine how losing Ms. Dinah would affect Mr. Everette. Although they were now in their seventies, Myles felt they still had some life to live. He kept his arm around Mr. Everette, consoling him, and praying that Ms. Dinah made it through.

A COUPLE OF HOURS LATER, A DOCTOR CAME FROM THE BACK AND called for Mr. Noble. Both men stood and cautiously approached the woman.

"Mr. Noble?" she confirmed, and he gave her a nod. "Your wife had a massive stroke. We tried everything we could." He sighed. "But we couldn't save her."

Mr. Everette's knees gave out, and were it not for Myles catching him, he would have hit the floor. He released a cry from deep within, and Myles could feel his agony. Once he was steady on his feet, Myles wrapped his arms around him and let him weep on his shoulder.

At some point, Myles was able to guide him over to their seats. Mr. Everette continued to shed tears as he spoke.

"She was my whole world," he sobbed. "What am I gonna do without her?"

"I don't know, Mr. Everette. You're a strong man, but nothin' could have prepared you for this. I know there's nothin' I can say that'll make this better. I'm sorry for your loss. Ms. Dinah was a great woman, and she meant a lot to me. Just know I'll be here for whatever you need."

As they sat quietly, not knowing what to do next, a nurse approached them.

"Sir?" They both gave her their attention. "If you would like a few moments with your wife—"

"I can't...not yet." He shook his head. "I need some time to process this, and I don't want to do this more than once. Can I wait for my daughter? She's flying in from Los Angeles. I umm—I don't know how long she'll be but—"

"No rush, Sir. We can take you to the family room for some privacy if you want," she offered.

"I'm good here. I want my daughter to be able to find me."

"Yes, Sir. I understand. Just let us know when you're ready. I'm truly sorry for your loss."

She reached for Mr. Everette's hand and gently squeezed it. He seemed to have gathered himself a bit. Myles's thoughts went to Everleigh and how devastated she would be when she heard the news. It pained him to know that another man would be helping her through this challenging time when he knew that it should be him. Shaking off the thought, he gave his focus back to Mr. Everette.

"Can I call somebody for you?" Myles offered, even though he knew that they didn't have much family.

Everette and Dinah were both the youngest of their siblings, and all of them had passed away over the years. They kept in contact with some of their nieces and nephews, but they weren't very close to any of them.

"No, I'll worry about that tomorrow," he replied solemnly.

"Okay. I'll be right back. Will you be okay for a few minutes?" He nodded.

Myles headed to the exit and pulled out his phone, calling his mom when he got outside.

"Hey, son. How are you?"

"I'm not so good, Ma. Ms. Dinah had a massive stroke. She ain't make it."

Myles had been keeping his tears at bay to be strong for Mr. Everette. But losing Ms. Dinah was a huge loss for him as well. As he spoke with his mom, he let a few tears fall from his eyes.

She gasped. "What? Oh no, Myles. I'm so sorry, son. How are Mr. Everette and Everleigh?"

"Leigh don't know yet. She's flyin' in from L.A. right now. It happened so fast, and it was unexpected. Mr. Everette is takin' it hard, Ma."

"I'm sure he is. How are you? I know Ms. Dinah was one of your favorite people. What do you need me to do? I'll get on a plane tomorrow and help any way I can."

"I'm good, Ma. It hurts, but I'm good. They both been so good to me all these years."

"They sure have, even though they didn't have to be. I'll look into some flights for tomorrow. I don't know if I can help, but my heart is telling me you need me there."

"Okay, and Ma, I know this ain't the time to be worried about this, but...I haven't seen Leigh since the day she left."

"You're right. This isn't the time to be worried about that. Just be there for her in whatever way she needs. She's gonna need all the support she can get."

"If she needs me, I'll be there."

"I know you will, and I'll be there tomorrow or the next day. I love you, son."

"Love you, too, Ma."

After ending the call, Myles went back inside to find Mr. Everette with his head leaning against the wall behind him, and his eyes closed. Myles sat down next to him, being careful not to disturb him. It would probably be a few hours before Everleigh arrived. He decided to rest his eyes, as well.

CHAPTER 5

Everleigh didn't have a good feeling in her gut, and for the past five hours, she prayed that it was wrong this time, although that was rare. She was beyond anxious and thought she'd never get to the hospital. When she arrived, she had the driver drop her off at the emergency room entrance. Inside, she looked around for her father and saw him sitting in the corner with...*Myles?*

If her main priority wasn't getting to her mother, she would have turned around and left. It had been over a decade since she laid eyes on him...and *damn* did he look good. She took a deep breath, then released it before she continued walking to where they were seated.

The two of them were in a deep conversation and didn't notice Everleigh coming their way. Myles looked up first and stopped talking mid-sentence, causing her father to follow his line of vision. Both men stood, and her father pulled her into his arms, while Myles looked on.

"Baby girl! I'm so glad you made it here safely," her father said, hugging her so tight, she could barely breathe.

"How's Ma?"

Her father took a step back but kept his arms on her shoulders.

Before he could say those dreadful words, Everleigh knew. Her gut was right, and she knew her mother was gone.

"Ev," her father said softly. "She's gone. She had a massive stroke, and they couldn't save her."

She buried her face in her father's chest again, and they cried about the loss of the woman they both loved more than themselves. Everleigh's mind went to all the great memories she had with her mother. Even though she lived on the other side of the country, she visited every other month and stayed for a week or more. Each visit, she spent quality time with her parents together and individually. She and her mother talked on the phone at least three times a day. With every thought that crossed her mind, she became more and more emotional.

Myles struggled to control his emotions as he watched two people that he loved, mourn the loss of someone they all loved. He could see that Mr. Everette was having a hard time consoling Everleigh because of his own emotions. The nurse that spoke with them earlier walked by, and Myles got her attention, then asked if they could be taken to the private room. When she agreed, he put his hand on each of their shoulders to get their attention.

"She's gonna take us to a private room, and once y'all ready, we can go see Ms. Dinah."

Everleigh looked at Myles and couldn't help but wonder how he ended up there but was glad that her father wasn't alone. They both gave him a nod, and the three of them followed the nurse to the room.

"Take as long as you need. When you're ready, push this button, and someone will come and take you to see your loved one."

"Thank you," I said.

Myles sat in a chair near the door, while Everleigh and her father sat on a small couch. Mr. Everette wore a solemn expression but was no longer crying, whereas his daughter couldn't seem to stop the tears.

"Daddy, tell me what happened. I just talked to Ma this morning and this afternoon, and she sounded fine."

Her father took her hands in his and explained the events of the day. Myles tried to remember if he noticed anything different about Ms. Dinah. To him, she seemed perfectly fine.

"You had dinner with my parents?" Everleigh asked him, looking at him with a slightly confused expression.

"He visits us often, Ev," Mr. Everette answered before Myles, then continued his recount the events of the evening. "After we finished eating, she said she had a headache and was tired. Myles offered to clean up the kitchen, so your mom could go rest. When he was getting ready to leave, we heard her fall."

Everleigh was still confused about Myles's relationship with her parents, but now wasn't the time to get answers about that.

"There were no signs? No warnings?"

"Nothing at all, baby girl. Everything after that happened so fast. I still can't believe she's gone."

"Me either, Daddy. I guess I'm ready to see her now."

Myles pushed the button that was on the wall next to where he was seated. Not even a full minute later, the same nurse returned and escorted them to see Ms. Dinah. Before she pushed the door open to the room, she stopped to say a few words.

"Again, take as much time as you need. We understand that this is very difficult. Once you're ready, we will discuss what needs to be done."

"Thank you," Myles told her again.

She pushed the door wide open and remained in front of it as they walked by, then closed it softly as she left. Everleigh went to the far side of the bed, while Mr. Everette went to the other side, and Myles stood at the foot.

"Dammit, Dinah! Why'd you have to leave me like this? You know I can't do shit without you." He leaned down and kissed his wife's forehead, then her lips. "I love you, woman. Always have, and I'll never stop. Our vows said until death do us part, but my love goes beyond the grave."

A few of his tears fell on her cheek, and he used his thumb to wipe them off. After a few moments of staring at his wife, he left the room.

Myles moved from the foot of the bed to where Mr. Everette had been standing. His hand went to Ms. Dinah's, and he noticed that she was still warm.

"Ms. Dinah, thank you for showin' me so much love over the years. I appreciate all the time we spent talkin' and the meals you made for me. Today, you even let a nigga know I made you proud. That shit means everything. My bad for cussin'. I'm gon' miss you."

He leaned down and kissed her forehead, then looked at her one more time before turning to leave the room.

"Wait!" Everleigh blurted out.

He turned back around, and their eyes met for the first time since she arrived.

"Stay with me," she whispered. "Please."

Without a moment of hesitation, he walked around to the other side of the bed and pulled Everleigh into his arms. She sank into his chest, putting her arms around his waist, and a fresh round of tears soaked his shirt.

"I'm so sorry, baby. I know this is hard," he said quietly, before kissing the top of her head.

"She's my best friend," she said through tears. "How am I gonna...we talk every day. Who am I gonna talk to now?"

Myles wanted to offer his friendship but knew that nothing could replace what she had with her mother. He had zero interest in being just her friend, anyway. He wanted much more than that. She continued to sob as she questioned what her life would be like without her mother.

"Last month, when I was home for a visit, she wanted to go bowling. I complained the whole way to the bowling alley. Even though neither of us could bowl, we ended up having the best time. We ate pizza and drank too much beer, then ended up having to call Daddy to pick us up because we were too tipsy."

She laughed through her tears as she told the story.

"When Daddy got there, he let us have it, told us we needed to grow up. He was so mad that he didn't even talk to us the next day."

As Everleigh recollected the last time she spent quality time with her mom, it reminded her of the feeling she had listening to her parents fuss back and forth while she laughed in the back seat. It was something they did all the time, but she knew there was nothing but love between them. She hoped that she and Easton could have a relationship like her parents had, but deep down, she knew they were missing something—a lot, actually.

Myles laughed at her memory, but still consoled her as much as he could. About ten minutes had passed when she finally released her hold on his waist and turned to face her mother again. As she held her hand, she spoke from her heart.

"Mommy, I can't believe you left me like this. You taught me everything but how to live without you. How, Mommy? How am I supposed to do this? How am I supposed to get married and have kids without you? This is so hard to accept, but you raised me to be strong, so I'll figure it out. Me and Daddy will figure it out together. I know you wouldn't want us to be sad. You'd want us to celebrate your life, and all the great times we had together. God couldn't have blessed me with a better mom, and I promise I won't be sad for long. I'll celebrate the thirty-four years I had with you. I love you, and I already miss you."

She leaned over her mother's body and hugged her as best she could, then kissed her cheek. When she turned around to face Myles, he was visibly shaken. The only people in the world that could get him to be so emotional was his mother, his baby sister, Myla, and Everleigh. Seeing Everleigh say her final goodbyes to her mother broke Myles's heart. They embraced again, but this time, it wasn't just Myles consoling her. This time, they comforted each other.

CHAPTER 6

Before leaving the hospital, arrangements were made for Ms. Dinah's body to be picked up by the funeral home. Mr. Everette didn't want to deal with anything else at that moment, so nobody forced him. By the time they arrived at the Noble residence, it was close to three in the morning.

Once they were inside, Mr. Everette went straight to the family room and turned on the television, and Everleigh followed.

"Daddy, the sun will be coming up soon. Don't you think you should get some rest?"

He adjusted the recliner so that he was lying back before replying.

"I'll be fine out here. I can't sleep in there tonight," was all he said.

She nodded her head in understanding, then grabbed the blanket that was on the couch, covering him with it, before kissing his cheek then going to the kitchen. Myles was leaning against the counter, drinking a bottle of water.

"I left your luggage by the door," he said.

"Thank you."

"Is he good? I mean..."

"I know what you mean. He doesn't want to sleep in the room without my mom."

"I can understand that."

For a few minutes, nothing was said. Although they hadn't seen or spoken to each other in over a decade, it didn't seem awkward to be in each other's presence. Everleigh often thought about what it would be like when she saw him again. The tragic circumstances of today's reunion took the focus away from having to discuss the past, at least for the time being.

Leaving Myles was probably one of the hardest things that Everleigh had ever done. She buried her feelings for him so deep that she almost had herself fooled about them not existing. All it took was one look at him to bring all those feelings back to the surface. She never stopped loving him. For a long time, she was pissed that he let her leave and never chased after her, though she only halfway expected him to.

Back then, Myles wasn't the type of nigga that would try to keep a woman that didn't want to be kept. Even though he was in love with Everleigh, like he told Mr. Everette, his pride got in the way. Today, he was a different man, and if he ever had another chance to have her again, he'd do anything to keep her in his life.

As Myles leaned against the counter, holding the water bottle he'd just emptied, he admired the woman who had his heart, the only woman he'd ever loved. He always thought that if he ever saw her again, he'd be angry, but all he felt was the love that remained when she disappeared.

She was a little thicker than he remembered, in all the right places, especially her thighs. The thought of burying his head between them had him adjusting his dick. Her medium brown skin was still as smooth and clear as it was the day they met when she was just eighteen years old. During the four years they spent together, she always wore her hair straight, but now, she sported her natural curls. He thought she was more beautiful than ever before.

Everleigh was sure she was going to hell when her time came. She couldn't believe that she was lusting over Myles at a time like this. As heavy as her heart was, her pussy was getting wetter by the minute.

The last time she'd seen him, he still had a hairless babyface and was sporting a curly fade. Now, his hair was in a perfectly lined Caesar cut with deep waves, that led into sideburns that connected to a sexy ass beard—the perfect seat. His skin looked like a smooth piece of dark chocolate, and Everleigh had to fight the urge she had to lick him. She smiled on the inside when she noticed him adjusting his dick.

"Leigh," she heard him say.

"Huh?"

"You good? I said your name three times."

"I, uhh, yeah. I'm okay. What were you saying?"

"I'm about to head out. I'll be back after I get a few hours of sleep."

He left the kitchen, tossing the water bottle in the container for recyclables on his way out, and headed toward the front door. Everleigh trailed behind him, taking in his physique. She was amazed at how good he looked. When he stopped and turned around, she almost ran into him, but he caught her and wrapped her in his arms. She took advantage of the moment, closing her eyes, inhaling his scent, and relaxing in his arms.

"You sure you good?" he asked her again. "I know today been hard, and you got some hard days ahead. I'm here for whatever you need, whenever you need me."

"I need you now," came out of her mouth before she could catch it.

Myles didn't reply because he didn't think he heard her right. He released her from the embrace and connected his eyes with hers. There was no need for her to repeat herself because they said it all. Taking a chance, Myles leaned down and kissed her lips.

He hadn't put his mouth on another woman's lips, neither set, since Everleigh left him. The kiss was so good, it tested the fuck out of his manhood, and he could have nutted right then and there. He was sure some precum had slipped out the tip of his dick. When he heard a deep moan, then realized it was him, he pulled away.

"Shit! My bad, Leigh. I, uhh—"

"It's okay. Don't go."

Myles tilted his head, questioning whether or not Everleigh knew what she was saying.

"Please," she continued. "Stay."

"Leigh, I don't know if that's a good idea. We both emotional as hell right now. I missed the fuck outta you, and I will fuck the shit outta you, in your father's house. I should go."

He turned around and opened the door. When he stepped onto the porch, he heard her say, "But you said whenever I need you."

Stopping in his tracks, he let his head fall and wondered why God was testing him this way. Turning to face her, he knew he couldn't deny her.

"I need you now," she pressed.

Giving in to her pleas, he nodded before saying, "If I was a grimy ass nigga, I'd take advantage of the emotional state that you in right now, but that ain't who I am. If I stay, we gotta chill, 'cause *when* I fuck you again, I need you to be in the right headspace."

Everleigh was turned on by how confident Myles was that they would have sex. He surely had reason to be because she was ready to bust it wide open for a real nigga right then.

"I just don't want to be alone."

"Let me go get my gym bag from the truck. I'll be right back."

When he returned, he locked up and turned on the alarm. As he headed toward the bedrooms, Everleigh was coming out of the family room.

"How is he?" Myles asked.

"He's asleep."

As he followed her to one of the guest rooms, Myles asked God to give him strength, because he knew that only He could stop him from sliding his dick deep inside of Everleigh's walls.

"I should probably go to the other room," he admitted, stopping in front of the door.

"Myles, please. I'm an engaged woman. I know how to control myself."

He crossed the threshold with a frown on his face, closing and locking the door behind him.

"You think I give a fuck about your engagement? If you were here under any other circumstances, my dick would already be in your chest."

Everything Myles said was doing something to Everleigh's body. She pretended to ignore his comments as he sat at the foot of the bed. He watched her as she moved around the room, taking things out of her suitcase and putting them in the drawers. He took off his shirt and tossed it on the bed before taking his duffle bag into the bathroom.

"I'm gon' take a quick shower," he told her, before closing the door.

While he showered, Everleigh continued unpacking, then checked her messages. It was then that it dawned on her that Easton hadn't reached out to her at all. He hadn't sent a single text or called to see how her mother was doing. Up until that moment, she had been willing to look past the obvious things that her relationship with Easton was missing. But his lack of concern about her mother's health was forcing her to reevaluate some things.

Easton was a very clean-cut, Carlton Banks kind of man and the complete opposite of Myles. Initially, that was what attracted Everleigh to him. It took her a long time to start dating again after she moved. At first, she was holding on to hope the Myles would come after her. Once she gave up on that dream, she decided it was time to date again. When she did, she realized that all the guys she was attracted to were replicas of Myles, including their chosen professions. Once she connected the dots based on their behavior and how they moved, she'd fall back.

After stepping away from the dating game for a few more years, she met Easton. She was doing a photo shoot for their company website, and they became friends. He was attracted to her from the beginning but didn't ask her out on a date until a few months later. After agreeing to the first date and several more, they just became a thing.

There were no sparks or butterflies, but Easton was attractive, charming, successful, and she felt comfortable around him. He seemed to be what she needed in her life at the time, and he and Myles had nothing in common. She didn't have to worry about him not coming home or getting a phone call that he'd been arrested or killed. That gave her comfort, and somehow, they fell into an easy relationship. Everleigh didn't even remember how it happened. He never officially asked her to be his girlfriend; she simply realized one day that she was.

After about a year of dating, he proposed, if that's what one would call it. Done without pomp and circumstance, Easton simply asked her if she wanted to get married one day. Of course, she replied with a yes, because she thought it was a general question. To her surprise, the next day, he came home with a big ass diamond ring. The little black box was sitting on her pillow one evening when she came home from a photo shoot. When she asked him what it was, he said, "Your engagement ring." He did, at least, put it on her finger.

"What an asshole," she whispered under her breath, or so she thought.

"Who's an asshole?" Myles said, startling her.

She looked up, and her breath hitched when she saw his naked chocolate chest. Her hand went to her own as she tried to gather herself, and not be so obvious that he was affecting her.

"Nobody. I was just, uhh, singing a song," she lied, as she put her phone away, deciding to deal with Easton in the morning.

Myles knew she was lying but didn't press the issue. As he walked past her, he knew she was staring at his dick print. He'd been hard since their first kiss in the hallway. He thought after he rubbed out a nut in the shower, his dick would soften. But he had a feeling that the only thing that would help would be releasing his seeds in Everleigh's mouth or womb. He knew he couldn't do either, so he wasn't sure how he'd make it the next few hours.

"I'm gonna shower," Everleigh told him.

By the time she walked back into the room, the lights were off. With the light from the bathroom, she could see that Myles was already in bed, lying on his back, on top of the comforter. After putting her things away, she turned off the bathroom light and grabbed the blanket from the foot of the bed. She got as close to him as possible, and he lifted his arm, allowing her to rest her head on his shoulder, then kissed the top of her head.

"Thank you for staying," she said quietly.

They both fell into a deep sleep, and despite the heavy events of the day, it was the best sleep either of them had gotten since the last night they spent together.

CHAPTER 7

T he next several days were a blur, but Everleigh was able to handle the funeral preparations better than she thought. There were moments when she would be overcome with sadness but understood that those moments would come and go. Her main concern was getting through the funeral and supporting her father.

Every night since he lost his wife, Everette slept in the family room, in the recliner. He couldn't bring himself to sleep in the bed that he'd shared with his wife for over fifty years. He was thankful that Everleigh was able to handle the arrangements, as difficult as it was, but he simply couldn't keep it together long enough to be of any help.

Without the support she received from Myles, Everleigh wouldn't have been able to get through the planning of or the days leading up to the funeral. He allowed her to cry in his arms when grief took over and reminisce about the good times when she felt like sharing. Everette found some comfort as he watched them together. He always knew that Myles was a standup guy and the man who was supposed to be by his daughter's side. If anything positive came from losing his wife, reuniting Myles and Everleigh would it.

When Everleigh spoke with Easton, the morning after her mother's death, he said a few comforting words before informing her that he wouldn't be able to come to Seattle until later in the week. Of course, Everleigh was pissed, but more than anything, she was hurt. She'd just lost her mother, and he couldn't put work to the side for a few days to support her.

When Everette inquired about Easton's whereabouts, all he was told was that he'd be there for the funeral. For all he cared, Easton could stay his bougie ass in L.A. A real man wouldn't allow his woman to experience such a traumatic event as losing her mother, and not go through hell or high water to be there for her. Everette already couldn't stand the man, and now, there was absolutely no hope of him ever liking him.

Myles wondered where Everleigh's fiancé was, as well. Not once during the time they spent together, did she bring him up. Since she thought it was important to mention that she was an 'engaged woman' and was still sporting that big ass rock on her finger, he assumed that she still had a fiancé. However, he was baffled by Easton's absence and lack of support as the woman he planned to spend the rest of his life with, prepared to bury her mother.

Myles's mom, Delilah, had been in town for a few days. As soon as she landed, she was prepared to help. While Myles and Everleigh ran funeral related errands, Delilah kept Mr. Everette company, and controlled the flow of traffic in and out of the house, as family and friends stopped by to offer their condolences and drop off food. Everleigh had been like a daughter to her when she was dating Myles, and her parents had treated him like a son, so she felt it was the least she could do.

The day of the funeral had arrived, and Myles decided to drive his truck. Everleigh didn't press him about it, so he figured her fiancé finally decided to show some support. His sister, Myla, along with her husband, Kolby, was in town to show their support. He was surprised to see them but appreciated them being there more than they knew. It couldn't have been easy for them to get away with twin toddlers and an infant at home.

When they arrived at the church, there was a small crowd out front. Delilah immediately saw some people that she knew and went to speak. Myles spotted Everleigh, as she stood next to her father, another man, and an older woman next to him. He assumed the man was Easton. He, Myla, and Kolby approached them and, not giving a single fuck, Myles walked up behind Everleigh and wrapped his arms around her waist.

The scent of his cologne made Everleigh forget that her fiancé was there. When she felt Myles's arms around her waist, she couldn't hide her smile. Turning around, she put her hands around his neck, and he buried his nose in hers, as they embraced. When they separated, Easton cleared his throat.

"You good?" Myles asked her, both of them ignoring Easton.

"I'm dreading it and wanting it to be over," she replied, not acknowledging Easton's vie for attention.

"It'll be over soon," Myles assured her, before kissing her forehead.

"Ev," Easton finally spoke.

She turned around to face him, and his expression was one of confusion. Since he'd arrived earlier that morning, Easton noticed how distant Everleigh had been. As much as he wanted to be there for her, he had some important deals that he needed to close before he left town. He assumed her attitude toward him was because he hadn't been there for her since her mother had passed away. But now, he wondered if this man, who she seemed inappropriately close to, was the reason.

"Myles, this is Easton—"

"Her fiancé," Easton finished the introduction for her, sticking his hand out.

"And this is Mrs. Briggs, Easton's mother," Everleigh continued.

Ignoring Easton, Myles greeted Mrs. Briggs properly, then stepped to the side so that he was no longer blocking Myla and Kolby.

"Oh my God! Myla, thank you so much for coming. You look amazing!"

The two ladies hugged before Myla replied, "So do you. I'm so sorry for your loss. From what I remember about your mom, she was an amazing lady."

"Thank you, and yes, she was. Who is this handsome gentleman?"

"This is my husband, Kolby. Baby, this is Everleigh."

"It's nice to meet you. I'm sorry for your loss." Kolby leaned in and hugged Everleigh.

"I'm Easton, her fiancé."

Myla and Kolby each shook his hand, earning a frown from Myles.

"My bad, Mr. Everette. You hangin' in there?" Myles said when he realized that he had yet to greet him.

Everette hadn't been looking forward to this day, but he had to admit, watching Easton squirm did bring him a bit of joy.

"I'm as good as to be expected, son."

Myles caught the look on Easton's face when Mr. Everette referred to him as 'son.' His discomfort was gonna be the highlight of Myles's day.

"You remember my sister, Myla. This is my brother-in-law, Kolby."

The couple greeted Mr. Everette and shared their condolences. After a few more minutes of mingling, it was time to go inside.

"Myles, you're sitting in the front with us. Dinah wouldn't have it any other way," Mr. Everette told him. "Have your mom come to the front as well."

"Of course. Whatever you want, sir."

If such a thing were possible, steam would be shooting out of Easton's ears. Everleigh had never mentioned anyone by the name of Myles, so he had no idea who this man was to her. Their level of comfort with each other led Easton to believe that they were more than friends, at least at some point. He began to wonder if her trips home were about more than seeing her parents, but he couldn't worry about that now. It was time to step and be the concerned and caring fiancé that he hadn't been all week.

The funeral for Dinah Leigh Noble was beautiful. It was indeed a celebration of her life, just as she would have wanted. As a former high school teacher, many of her students were present, and some gave remarks. It was wonderful to see the positive impact she had on so many people. Everleigh and her father shed a lot of tears, but mostly, they were tears of joy.

The pastor gave one last call for remarks, and Everleigh was surprised when Myles stood and approached the podium. All week, she wanted to ask him about his relationship with her parents. When he interacted with her father, it was evident that they were close. Every time she wanted to bring it up, there were more pressing matters that needed to be dealt with.

"Good morning, and God bless. I don't have a lot to say because I'd rather be doin' anything else right now than sayin' my final goodbye to this amazin' woman. Y'all don't know me, so I guess I should introduce myself. My name is Myles, and a long time ago, I dated Ms. Dinah's daughter, Everleigh."

He looked in Everleigh's direction, who already had tears in her eyes, and he couldn't help but notice how vexed Easton looked.

"From day one," he continued, "Ms. Dinah treated me like a son...her and Mr. Everette did. Even after Leigh and I broke up, Ms. Dinah poured into me, lifted me up, encouraged me, and loved me, despite some of the decisions I made in life. I'm grateful that I was able to tell her, before she passed away, how much I appreciated the role she played in me becomin' a man. I'm gonna miss the talks we had over dinner, but mostly, I'm gonna miss her presence. I know that I'm a better man because of this woman, and I'm thankful that even though things didn't work out between me and Leigh, she thought enough of me to keep me in her life. Thank you."

By the time Myles was done, Everleigh was sobbing uncontrollably. She had no idea that her parents had maintained such a close relationship with Myles after they broke up. Neither of them ever mentioned it. Her father put his arm around her shoulders and let her cry it out. Easton couldn't bring himself to give her any comfort because he couldn't determine if the tears were for her mother or Myles.

THE DAY HAD FINALLY COME TO AN END. THE FUNERAL, BURIAL, and repast were over, and Everleigh and her father were at home. Myles took his family to the airport after the burial, and Everleigh wondered if he would be stopping by later that night. She understood that he was keeping his distance, with Easton being in town. But she had to admit, after spending so much time together the past week, she missed him.

Everleigh and her father sat in the family room, watching an episode of *Sanford & Son*. Neither of them was paying it very much attention because they were lost in their thoughts. Suddenly, Everette broke the silence.

"I know it's been final since she took her last breath, but now that we've had the funeral, it feels..." He shook his head. "I don't know what I'm trying to say, baby girl."

"It's okay, Daddy. I know what you mean."

"This week has been so busy. People in and out of the house, phone ringing constantly. Now that she's buried, all that will stop and people will move on with their lives. They won't be worried about me."

"Oh, Daddy," Everleigh cried as she stood and went to the recliner, where he was seated.

She put her arms around his neck before saying, "You'll have me. I'll be here as long as you need me, and so will Myles. I know it's not the same as Ma, but you won't be alone."

"Eventually, I will. I don't expect you to put your life on hold forever. You have a fiancé and a career in L.A. I'm glad to have you here for as long as you can stay, but I know it won't be forever."

She hugged him a little longer, then kissed his cheek before going back to the couch. The thought of leaving her father alone in that house made her feel sad. She knew that he was right and that she would have to get back to her life, but she didn't want to think about that right now. Knowing that he had Myles did give her some comfort.

"Daddy, when did you and Ma get so close to Myles? I mean, I know you both liked him a lot when we were together, but how did that relationship evolve after we broke up?"

"We ran into him at the grocery store a couple of months after you left. Dinah invited him over for dinner, and we told him he was welcome to come over any time. At first, he didn't come very often. I don't think he was comfortable. After a while, though, sometimes he'd stop by just to talk, sometimes he'd come cut the grass, other times, he'd bring us groceries, or fix things around the house. He's been as much of a blessing to us as he feels we were to him. I think being close to us made him feel close to you. That man still loves you, you know."

Everleigh knew that Myles still loved her, and she felt the same way about him.

"Why didn't you say anything?"

"None of us were sure how you'd feel about it, so we decided not to mention it. Does that upset you?"

She shook her head. "No, I understand. It would've been awkward, especially when we first broke up and probably even more after Easton and I got engaged."

At the mention of Easton's name, Everette's expression changed, and his daughter noticed.

"Daddy, why don't you like Easton?"

"I have a better question...why do you?"

"Easton is a nice, successful, attractive man. He—"

"He clearly doesn't put you and your feelings first. Your mother died suddenly, and he couldn't even put his work on hold to be by your side. A man...a real man would never leave you alone to mourn a loss like that. I barely liked him as it was, but now, there's no chance of that ever happening. If he's who you choose to be with, I can be cordial. But that's where it ends."

"But Daddy, he—"

"But Daddy, nothing. Whatever he had going on could have been put on hold for a few days. I know he runs a big company, and that's all fine and good. If you want to spend the rest of your life with a man who can't put you first, it's your decision to make. But don't be surprised when he doesn't make you and the family you might have a priority."

Everleigh didn't have a rebuttal. She knew her father was right and was finally ready to accept it. Silence filled the room again, and eventually, Everette dozed off. Everleigh decided to go out to the porch and sit on the swing that her parents had installed a few years ago. There was a cool breeze blowing, so she took a light blanket with her. As she enjoyed the quiet of the evening, she thought about everything her father said and wondered where Easton was.

He and his mother had booked a room at a hotel and went there after the repast. He planned to go to the house to spend some time with Everleigh while his mother stayed back at the hotel. As soon as Shelby got her son alone, she let him have it. Just as Easton noticed the connection between Everleigh and Myles, so did she.

"You may have lost the best thing that ever happened to you. Did you see how her and her ex looked at each other? I knew you were making a huge mistake, not coming to be with her as soon as possible."

"Mom, please. Everleigh loves me, and her ex is old news. Yes, I used poor judgment by not coming sooner, but I think she understands."

Shelby looked at her son from the passenger seat and shook her head.

"Who raised you? I swear to God, all of your craziness came from your father's side of the family. Your fiancée's mother died, and you didn't show up until the day of the funeral. Son, tell me where you think that would be acceptable?"

"You know how important those closings were. We'd been going back and forth for weeks—"

"Then another week wouldn't have hurt. You really need to get your priorities straight. I won't be surprised if Everleigh breaks off the engagement and goes right back to her ex. I know I sure as hell would."

Easton wanted to respond to his mother, but something told him that she was right. He and his mother had always been close, and she'd always been supportive of him. However, she also didn't have a problem being honest with him either. The remainder of the ride to the hotel was in silence. He knew he was on Everleigh's shit list but hoped to smooth things over when he saw her again. There was no way he could go back to L.A. with them on bad terms, especially with her ex lurking around.

When he parked in front of the Noble residence, he saw Everleigh sitting on the porch. She was so deep in her thoughts that she didn't notice his presence until he sat on the swing.

"Shit! You scared me."

"Why are you sitting out here in the dark, not paying attention to your surroundings?" Easton questioned.

"I got a lot on my mind," she replied.

"Oh? Like what?"

He tried to put his arms around her shoulders and pull her into his side, but she resisted. When she didn't respond, he knew she had an attitude.

"What's on your mind?"

"You."

"Okay. Is that a good or a bad thing?"

"What do you think? My mom died a week ago, and today is the first time I've seen you."

"I figured you were upset about me not coming sooner. Look at me." She adjusted her body so that she was facing him. "Ev, you gotta know that if I could've been here sooner, I would have. What I was working on couldn't be pushed back."

"It doesn't feel like I'm a priority to you."

"What? Of course, you are. You mean more to me than anything. Why would you say that?"

"It's your family's company, and you're trying to tell me you couldn't put your work on hold for a few days. You should have been here, Easton. I don't care what you had going on. You should have dropped everything and been by my side. My mother died!"

She got up from the bench and paced back and forth, with her arms folded across her chest. Instead of using that moment to apologize and show that he cared, he got on the defensive.

"From what I could see, you had plenty of support from your ex."

Easton had been waiting for the perfect moment to bring up Myles. The way they hugged each other, right in front of him, at the church made him uneasy. He could tell by the way they looked at each other that there was something there. In the three years that he and Everleigh had been together, she'd never looked at him that way.

"Really, Easton? Had you been here, there wouldn't have been any room for Myles to offer his support. You left that door wide the fuck open."

"Did you open your legs as wide?"

As soon as the words came out of his mouth, he regretted it. Everleigh stopped pacing and marched toward him.

"What the fuck did you just say to me?"

Easton couldn't figure out how to clean up what he'd just said, and now he was in a worse position than he was before he arrived.

"I'm just saying. He seemed mighty comfortable hugging all over you, as if your fiancé wasn't standing there, and you didn't stop him."

He was making this a lot easier than she thought it would be.

"So, now a friendly hug equates to fucking? You know what?" She lifted her hand and waved her engagement ring in his face. "Go! Take your ass, and this ring on. I'm done with you and this conversation."

She slid the ring off and pushed it into his chest before stomping away, but just as she reached the front door, Easton roughly grabbed her arm.

"Wait!"

She looked down at their connection, and he quickly released his hold.

"Don't leave. I'm sorry, baby. Come back and sit down, so we can talk."

"Easton, there's not a lot to talk about. This past week, you've shown me who you are, and I don't like what I see. During the hardest time in my life, you went ghost on me. What's the saying, 'when people show you who they are, believe them the first time'?"

"Damn, Ev! I do one thing wrong, and you're ready to call it quits? It makes me wonder how you really feel about me if you can let go that easily."

"This isn't the first time you've shown me how selfish and self-centered you are. For some reason, I chose to ignore it, but now, I've seen enough to know that it's time for me to move on. This was one *big* thing, so you made it easy to let go."

Again, she tried to go into the house, but Easton stopped her.

"I'm sorry, Ev. I really am. I'll let you have some time and give you some space, but we're not over. I'll make this up to you, I promise."

He kissed her forehead before she went back inside. As she showered, she thought about the past three years with Easton. She could admit they shared some good times. If nothing else, they were good friends. Maybe that was the problem; she thought of him as a good friend that she had average sex with regularly.

Three years is a long time to be with someone and not feel *something* for them. She loved Easton, but she was never head over heels in love with him. Romantically something was missing, and she knew they didn't have what it took to have everlasting love like her parents had, and she was ready to accept it.

When Easton got back to his suite, his mother came knocking. She'd been listening out for him. He wanted to ignore her, but he knew she wouldn't go away.

"You're back early," she said, as soon as he opened the door.

"Everleigh had a long day. She wanted to get some rest."

"Will you be stopping by to see her tomorrow before we leave? I'd like to see her."

"Umm, yeah. We planned to have breakfast," he lied.

"Good. So, I take it she forgave you for your absence this week."

As she spoke, he began to empty his pockets, putting the contents on the table, when Everleigh's engagement ring slipped out and landed on the carpet. Of course, it caught his mother's eyes.

"I guess that answers my question," she said, her voice full of disappointment.

"It's not what you think. We're just taking a break. I'll give her some time to—"

"Get back with her ex...because that's exactly what's about to happen. I tried to tell you, but your hardheaded ass refused to listen."

She headed toward the door, as she shook her head and mumbled under her breath, probably saying, "I told you so."

Sleep didn't come easy for Easton that night. Thoughts of Everleigh with Myles plagued his mind. He didn't want to believe that she would move on from him so quickly, but he couldn't deny the obvious connection that she had with her ex.

CHAPTER 8

After Myles dropped his family off at the airport, he wanted to stop by Mr. Everette's house to see how he and Everleigh were doing. However, since her fiancé was in town, and Myles had retired from taking lives, he went home and took a nap. It was a good ass nap, too. He dreamed about the last time he made love to Everleigh, the day before she left him. It was a vivid dream because he had it often.

She had just come in from a photography class that she was taking at Seattle Central Community College. He hadn't come home the night before and didn't make it in until after she'd left for class. She walked into their bedroom just as he came out of their bathroom. With a towel wrapped around his waist, his dick was swinging with every step he took toward her, causing the towel to open slightly. He knew she was pissed because she hadn't responded to any of his texts or phone calls that morning.

When he reached her and leaned in to kiss her lips, Everleigh leaned away, causing Myles to smirk. Reaching up and grabbing her by the back of her neck, he pulled her back toward him and planted a big, juicy kiss on her lips. When he released her, she placed both of her hands on his naked chest and pushed him as hard as she could. He didn't even budge.

"*Don't kiss me! I don't know where the fuck your lips been all night!*"
Myles cocked his head to the side and frowned up his face.

"*Leigh, don't play with me. I might do a lot of shit, but fuckin' another bitch ain't one, and you know damn well I ain't puttin' my mouth on nobody but you.*"

"*How the fuck am I supposed to know that? You didn't bring your ass home until after nine o'clock this morning. What am I supposed to think?*"

"*You ain't supposed to think shit. You should know I love your ass more than life. I might be out in these streets hustlin', but I don't do shit to disrespect you or our relationship.*"

"*You being out all night is disrespectful, Myles. I'm sick of this shit.*"

Myles blew out a deep breath. He was tired of having the same argument with her. It was literally the only thing they ever argued about. He heard her complaints loud and clear and was making some moves to go legit, but he needed her to be a little more patient.

"*Baby, I know you tired, I swear I do. It might not seem like it, but I hear you. Okay?*"

This time, when he tried to kiss her lips, she didn't resist. As they kissed, he wrapped her in his arms, moving his hands down to grope her ass, and as usual, she melted. Everleigh wanted to believe that he heard her, but the longer it took for him to leave the streets, the less she believed he was doing anything to make it happen.

His hands moved around to the front of her body, where he unbuttoned and unzipped her jeans with ease. Sticking his hands into the back of her panties, he pushed them and the jeans down over her ass and half of her thighs. Everleigh assisted him with getting them off the rest of the way. The towel he had around his waist had already fallen to the floor.

Once she was out of her shirt and bra, he picked her up, and she wrapped her legs around his waist. Slowly, they eased down to the bed, and when he was comfortably on top of her, he looked in her eyes.

"*I'm tryin' to get this shit right so you'll marry a nigga. Promise not to give up on me.*"

"*Okay.*"

"*You promise?*"

"*I promise,*" *Everleigh lied.*

Myles believed the lie because he refused to believe anything else. He didn't know that when his tongue played with her chocolate nipples, that it would be the last time. He didn't know that when he buried his face between her thighs, that it would be last time he'd indulged in her succulent sweetness. He had no idea that when she wrapped her lips around his dick, that it would be the last time the tip would touch her tonsils. He didn't have a clue that when he entered her tight, slippery haven, that it would be the last time they brought each other to ecstasy.

When he woke up, his dick was hard as hell. He thought about calling Nyema but decided against it. A substitute wouldn't do right now. She'd been blowing his phone up this past week, and if he called now, he would have to let her know that shit between them was over. They'd been fucking around for a long time, and he respected her enough to not tell her some shit like that over the phone. He knew he needed to deal with that sooner rather than later, but today wasn't the day.

He quickly jumped in the shower and used his hand to bust two nuts, before bathing. He wasn't satisfied in the least, but it would have to do. After getting dressed, he went to get something to eat. The plan was to pick up his food and head back home, but somehow, his truck was headed to the Noble residence. When he arrived, he noticed a car that didn't belong to them in front of their house, so he parked a few houses down.

Myles could clearly see Everleigh and her nigga on the porch, sitting on the bench, and he didn't feel bad for watching them. They looked to be in a deep conversation, and he wished he could hear them, but he was too far away. Everleigh finally went inside, leaving Easton on the porch. A few minutes later, he hopped in the car that was parked in front of the house and left.

Myles parked in the same spot a minute later, then, for the first time, used the key that Mr. Everette gave him to let himself in. Locking the door behind him, he walked further into the house. He could hear the TV in the family room, and since it was late, he figured Mr. Everette was asleep in the recliner. Making his way to Everleigh's room, he slowly turned the knob and entered. The bathroom door was half-closed, and the shower was running, so Myles sat in the sofa chair in the corner of the room.

Everleigh came out of the bathroom with a towel wrapped around her body and her hair. Her eyes got big when she saw Myles, but she wasn't startled.

"What are you—how did you get in here?" she asked.

"I have a key."

Her father had made it clear that Myles was family—*but a damn key to the house?*

"You have a key to my parents' house? That's—"

"It's for emergencies, but this is the first time I've used it," he explained.

"Was there an emergency?"

"I wanted to see you."

She nodded her head, then gathered her pajamas, and went back in the bathroom. When she returned, she had on a tank top and a pair of loose-fitting shorts, with her hair still wrapped in the towel. Positioning herself at the head and center of the bed, against the headboard, she sat with her legs crisscrossed, covering them with a blanket. Myles kept his eyes on her while she made herself comfortable.

"How you been?" he asked her.

"It's been a long day but—"

"Naw, I know today was hard. I'm glad you got through it. I wanna know how you been since you left me?"

Well, let's get right to it then. "Oh...I've been...good. You?"

"Fucked up," he replied without hesitation.

She was taken aback by his honesty and didn't know how to respond. The pain in Myles's voice was evident. He couldn't hide it if he tried. Everleigh had no idea how much she'd hurt him, but she was about to find out.

"Oh, I, umm..."

"It's cool, Leigh. You did what you had to do. It fucked me up and, real talk, I'm still fucked up about it. I'm happy for you, though. It seems like you been livin' your dream."

Everleigh didn't respond right away, taking a moment to reflect on whether or not she was truly living her dream. On a professional level, that was definitely the case, but personally, there was a lot to be desired.

"I wouldn't say I've been living my dream."

"Why? You got the career you always wanted, livin' in L.A., engaged to a man I assume you love. What's missin'?"

"You," came out of her mouth, barely above a whisper.

Her hand went over her mouth because she couldn't believe she'd let that slip out. However, what she didn't know was that she'd just given Myles the green light to move full force ahead.

"It's too late now. You can't take it back. Tell me how you feel."

Everleigh shook her head. "It just slipped out. I—I'm—"

"So, you ain't mean what you said?"

"Yeah, I mean, I, shit—"

Myles was making her nervous, and she couldn't put together a sentence if she tried. The feelings she thought were buried were front and center, ready to be acknowledged, even if she wasn't quite prepared to do so.

"I guess you ain't figured this shit out yet, so let me tell you wassup. You're mine, Leigh. I let you walk outta my life once already, but that shit won't happen again."

He stood from the chair and took slow, but deliberate steps toward the bed. Everleigh's breathing picked up, the closer he got. Stopping at the foot of the bed, he continued.

"I love you, Leigh. I never stopped. I shouldn't have let you go so easily, but my pride had me all fucked up. You *promised* me you wouldn't give up on me, and the next day, *the very next day*, *Leigh*, your ass was in the wind. That shit *hurt*. It hurt like hell. You broke your promise to me, right when I was so close to fulfillin' my promise to you. You gave up on me, right when I was ready to prove to you that I was worthy of your love."

Tears fell from Everleigh's eyes as Myles poured out his heart. She had no idea she'd hurt him so deeply. All this time, she thought he didn't care. He never tried to call, text, email, or reach out in any way, after she left.

"But you know what happened? Instead of goin' through with my plan, the plan I had for us, I went right back to what I knew best. Why not, huh? I ain't have you. I got so deep in that shit." He shook his head as he thought about it. "I know the only reason I'm still here is because of God, and the prayers of my mother and sister, and your parents."

She crawled to the foot of the bed and sat with her legs on either side of his. The bed was high enough that she could wrap her arms around his waist and rest her head on his stomach.

"Myles, I'm so—so sor—sorry," she cried. "I didn't want to leave. I swear I didn't. I just didn't—I didn't know you were listening."

One of his hands went to rub her back softly. He removed the towel on her head with the other, before burying his fingers in her damp hair.

"Baby, I'm not sayin' this shit to make you feel bad. I'm tellin' you because I need you to know that you hurt a nigga, *to my core*, but I *still* love you. I never stopped lovin' you."

She sat back a little and looked up at him, with tears still falling from her eyes. Cupping her face in his hands, he used his thumb to wipe them away.

"Why'd you wait so long to tell me?" she asked.

"At first, I was mad, then I was hurt, then I thought you might be better off without me. I thought you were happy, and if that was the case, I love you enough not to fuck up your happiness."

"How do you know I'm not happy now?"

"Because I can see it in your eyes. I saw it the first time our eyes connected in Ms. Dinah's hospital room."

Everleigh tried to look away, but Myles used his index finger to lift her chin.

"Tell me."

"Tell you what?"

"Are you happy?"

"It depends on what we're talking about," she replied.

"Oh, so you wanna get specific. That's cool. Are you happy with that nigga?"

"I'm...I'm content. Or at least I was up until recently."

"Content ain't happy, baby. That shit ain't even close. But since you don't wanna admit it, straight up, tell me this."

Covering her mouth with his, he pushed his tongue between her lips, finding hers ready and waiting to connect with his. He didn't realize how much he missed kissing until that moment. As soon as he heard her moan, he pulled away.

"He make you feel like that from a simple kiss?"

She answered with a breathy, "No."

He leaned downed to kiss her again, and as their tongues intertwined, he lifted her from the bed. Wrapping her legs around his waist and gripping her ass, he began a slow grind against her pussy. Grinding had never felt so good to either of them, and it was better than any sex they'd had since the breakup. This time, he moaned, some shit he didn't normally do, and it brought him back to the reality of what was happening. Detaching his mouth from hers and releasing the hold he had on her ass, Everleigh fell back on the bed. He took two steps back and stared down at her, debating on his next move. His dick was hard as hell, as it rested against his pelvic area. He could feel precum seeping onto his stomach, underneath the T-shirt he was wearing.

Everleigh was breathing hard and fast. Her nipples were like pebbles and could be seen through her tank top. She squeezed her thighs together, trying to calm the ache between them. No man had ever made her feel the way Myles did. Her pussy was already wet and had been for some time. As she thought about the way Myles's lips and tongue felt against hers, and the way his erection felt as he ground against her mound, she wanted more.

You would think that she hadn't had sex in months, but that wasn't the case. She and Easton had sex often. The problem was, the shit was so...vanilla. So she hadn't had great sex since she left Myles. You know, that kind of sex that makes your pussy throb just thinking about it. The type of sex that has your toes curling and your legs cramping. Easton didn't even like her to suck or ride his dick. He barely wanted to hit it from the back. *Now what kinda shit was that?* And eating pussy...*ha*! He didn't mind doing it, but he was so horrible at it, most times, Everleigh declined. If it weren't for her many vibrators, she would rarely have orgasms.

Myles wanted to make love to Everleigh, but he knew that the first time he entered her, after twelve years, would be nothing but fucking. He'd already begun to mentally prepare himself for the quick nut he knew he would bust. Everleigh was getting impatient. She was anxious to feel him stretching her walls. Since he seemed to need a little encouragement, she shimmied out of her shorts and tank top, then opened her legs...wide.

"Come get this wet ass pussy, baby."

He admired her frame and took note of the way her body had matured. Everleigh had become a grown-ass woman during their time apart. She even had a few stretch marks on the sides of her stomach and her hips from the weight that she'd gained. Myles loved her new body.

She used the pads of two of her fingers to rub her clit and pushed the same two fingers on her other hand into her already dripping hole. When he noticed that her ring was missing, his dick got harder, and a big smile graced his face.

"Shit," he said. "I ain't even have to tell you to get rid of that nigga."

"It's over with him...and I'm yours if that's what you want."

"Is that what you want?"

"More than anything."

He slipped out of his shirt and shoes at the same time. When he pushed down his sweats and underwear, his dick popped out, and almost poked him in his chin when he bent to take off his socks. He couldn't tear his eyes away from her pleasuring herself. Gripping his dick, he began to stroke up and down, then around the tip.

Everleigh's mouth began to salivate at the sight of it. She hadn't forgotten how long and thick it was, and how it curved upward and to the right, just a little bit. She remembered how deep it went and how it felt as if it was touching the depths of her soul. As bad as she wanted to taste him, it would have to wait. She wanted to feel him first.

"Give it to me," she pleaded.

"Did you let that nigga in my pussy raw, Leigh?"

She shook her head. "No, never."

Myles continued to stroke his growing erection. "You let *anybody* in my shit raw, Leigh?"

"Nobody."

"You ain't lyin' just to get the dick, are you?"

"I swear, only you hit raw. Please, give it to me."

Everleigh was telling the truth. After her and Easton got engaged, he thought she would loosen her stance about him using condoms, but she never did. Even after they got tested together, she refused.

"Put your fingers in your mouth and tell me how good that pussy taste."

She brought her hand to her mouth, then sucked each finger individually, moaning louder with each one. Finally, Myles lined his dick up with her hole, and as he slowly entered her, he kissed her lips, then sucked on her tongue, savoring the taste of her heavenly fluids. Once his entire length was submerged inside of her, he stilled. He wanted to enjoy the feeling of her tongue against his and relish in her flavor.

Everleigh couldn't take it anymore. Even though he wasn't moving, the curve of his dick was hitting the right spot. She was on the brink of climaxing, and he had yet to give her one good thrust. When her pussy began to tighten around his dick, Myles pulled his entire length out, leaving only the tip in, then slammed it back inside.

"Ahh, shit!" Everleigh screamed.

"Shh, baby. You can't be too loud."

The more he pumped, the louder she got, so he covered her mouth with his to stifle her moans. However, all kissing did was bring his nut to the surface and it felt so fucking good, Mr. Everette was about to get an earful if he was awake.

"Fuck, Leigh! I missed you so much."

"I missed you, too, baby. Oh, shit! I'm cu-cu-cummming!"

Myles quickened his strokes while coaxing her nut out. "Gimme my shit, baby. I want twelve years' worth of juice on shit."

"Oh my damn! This feels so fuckin' good, baby. God, I love you, Myles. I love you so much."

That did it for him. Hearing her say those words pulled his nut right on out, and he filled her with his seeds. Pulling out didn't even cross his mind.

"Aghhh, fuucckkk! I love you, Leigh."

CHAPTER 9

T he following morning when Everleigh woke up, she could sense that Myles was gone. When she tried to sit up, the soreness in her body reminded her of the fantastic night they spent together. As she leaned against the headboard, she saw a note on the pillow next to her.

Morning Beautiful. Since you ain't gave a nigga your number yet, here's mine. Save me as 'My Nigga'.

She wore a big ass smile on her face as she saved her nigga's number in her phone, then sent him a text.

Me: You my nigga now?

My Nigga: What that contact say?

Me: Whatever

My Nigga: What that pussy say?

Me: Boy bye!

As Everleigh was about to put her phone back on the bedside table, a call came in. She was cheesing again when she saw who it was.

"Hey," she answered.

"How that pussy feel?"

"What kinda greeting is that, Myles?"

"That kinda you get when I wanna know how that pussy feel."

"Oh my God. You still nasty as hell."

"What? You thought I was gon' change?"

"You're almost forty. It's possible."

"You know you like that shit, so stop talkin' crazy. Come have lunch with me."

"Lunch? What about breakfast?"

"Shit, if you wanna have breakfast for lunch. That's cool, but it's lunchtime."

Everleigh moved the phone away from her ear and looked at the screen.

"Oh, damn! It's almost noon. How the hell am I still in this bed?"

"Give yourself a break, Leigh. It's been a tough week. Yesterday was a lot, and I know I wore that pussy out."

"You know what? I'm about to hang up on your nasty ass."

"I'll text you the address."

Myles hung up before Everleigh could respond. Before getting out of bed, she checked her other messages and saw that she had a few from Easton.

EB: Can we meet for breakfast before I leave?

EB: I know you're upset, but don't I deserve a reply.

EB: Fine! I said I'd give you some time and space.

Although she wasn't ready to talk to him, she felt bad that she didn't see his texts until it was too late. She wouldn't have met up with him, but she would have replied to his texts. Going through the rest of her messages, she saw that her only two friends in Los Angeles had messaged her again. Since the day Everleigh gave them the news, they'd been checking on her daily, but she had been too busy to respond. Instead of replying to their text messages, she decided to FaceTime them both.

"Evyyyyy, I'm so sorry for your loss, sis. I know you and your mom were close, and you must be devastated. I've been calling and texting you since I found out, but I figured you were overwhelmed with everything. I sent flowers, did you get them?" Layne said as soon as she picked up the phone.

Everleigh and Layne met at an event that she had been hired to photograph. They literally ran into each other because Everleigh was trying to get a good shot. After she apologized for almost knocking Layne off her feet, they hit it off and had been friends since.

"I know, Lay. I saw all of your texts and listened to your messages. It's been crazy, but I appreciate your concern. I'm sure we got the flowers, but honestly, I have no idea."

"It's cool, sis. I know how it is. When my mom died, I didn't know if I was coming or going that first week. It's not something you ever get over, but you'll learn to deal."

"Yeah, I can see that already. My mom lived a full, happy life with the man of her dreams. I get sad, and I miss her so much already, but I would surely get an earful if she knew I was sitting around crying and shit."

"Well, don't. It won't bring her back, and you'll just end up with a headache. You'll have some weak moments for sure, and you need to let yourself have them but celebrate her life as much as you can. I know she would prefer that."

"She would. Thank you, Lay. Now, let me call Robbie. Hold on."

Everleigh went through the steps to merge the FaceTime calls, and Robbie's face appeared at the bottom of her screen. Robbie and Layne had been friends since high school, so she met her through Layne.

"Ev, my goodness! We've been trying to reach you. How are you, sis?"

"I'm good. I mean, I'm dealing."

"That's all you can do," Robbie replied. "I didn't want to bug you too much, but I wanted you to know I was thinking about you."

"Thank you, Rob. I swear I wasn't ignoring y'all."

"Girl, we never thought that. But wait a minute...Layne, do you see what I see, or are my eyes deceiving me."

"Robbie, I noticed some shit when she first called me, but I ain't wanna say nothing," Layne answered with a huge grin.

"What are y'all talking about?"

"We don't know, Ev. Tell us why you got a glow that's screaming *well-fucked*," Robbie said, causing Everleigh to gasp. "And your hair looks like somebody had a nice grip on it last night or in the wee hours of the morning. Hell, maybe both," Robbie added.

Everleigh put her fingers in her hair and felt around.

"Don't try to fix it now. You been found out. Oh, and I ain't sure, but it looks like *somebody* wanted to mark their territory. Robbie, are those hickies on her neck?"

Everleigh's hand went to her neck as if she could feel them. When she tried to hop out of bed to go to the bathroom, the soreness between her legs slowed her down.

"Ah, shit!" she groaned as she waddled to the bathroom.

"Mmmhmm, I think our friend has some explaining to do," Robbie teased.

When Everleigh made it to the bathroom and looked in the mirror, her eyes got wide. Everything her girls had mentioned was staring her in the face. Myles left her with a well-fucked glow, after-sex hair, and marks all over her neck.

"I'm gonna strangle him," she finally said.

"Him?" her friends chimed simultaneously.

"Who is *him?*" Robbie continued.

"Because I know *him* ain't Easton's ole non-fuckin' ass. He's *never* left you looking this thoroughly fucked," Layne added.

"More like barely fucked," Robbie said with a laugh.

"So, who is he, Ev?" Layne pressed.

"Umm, well, see—" Everleigh began.

"Oh—my—God! Did you finally *cheat* on Easton?"

"No, I didn't *cheat* on Easton," she paused. "We broke up."

"What?"

"Are you serious?"

They both spoke in shocked tones at the same time.

"Are y'all really that surprised? Y'all been saying I should end things since he proposed."

"I don't know why you insist on calling that whack ass proposal a proposal," Robbie fussed.

"You know what I mean."

"Unfortunately, we do. Tell us what happened and who you already replaced him with."

Everleigh told them about her breakup with Easton, and neither of them were surprised by his lack of support. Of course, they had to add their two cents and pointed out different times during their relationship that Easton wasn't supportive, things that Everleigh had let slide.

"Ev, Easton is a nice guy, and he's fine as hell, but we've been telling you from the beginning that he wasn't the man for you," Layne reminded her. "A blind man could see there was no passion between you two."

"And he's spoiled, selfish, jealous, and real talk, kinda controlling. Not overly, but I've caught glimpses of it," Robbie added.

They didn't hide their satisfaction about her breakup with Easton, that was for sure. Everleigh went on to tell them as little about Myles as she could, keeping it short and sweet.

"He was my first love, and circumstances pulled us apart. We hadn't seen each other since I moved to L.A. twelve years ago."

"Oh, wow. No wonder you look thoroughly fucked—because you got thoroughly fucked. He wants that old thang back, so he had to dig them guts out to remind you what you left behind," Robbie teased.

"Aww, Ev. You're the one that got away. This could have such a beautiful ending," Layne cooed.

"Possibly, but I gotta go. He wants to have lunch."

"Okay. Call us when you can. Love you.

"Love you."

"Love y'all, too."

Everleigh ended that call, then showered and dressed as quickly as her sore body would let her. She chose a pair of skinny jeans, a black graphic T-shirt with Lauryn Hill on the front, and a pair of black wedge sandals. She wet her hair in the shower and managed to get it in a puff on the top of her head. After adding some lip gloss, she left her room and bumped into her father.

"Oh, I'm sorry, Daddy. I didn't see you." She stood on her toes and kissed his cheek.

"It's okay. I was just about to check on you. It's not like you to sleep this late."

"I know, Daddy. I was umm...up late, so I was exhausted."

"Did you and Myles finally sort things out? I saw him leaving this morning."

"Huh? Oh, you—you saw Myles?"

"Yeah. We talked a bit before he left. He had to get to his shop since he was closed yesterday."

"His shop?"

A smirk appeared on Everette's lips, and he couldn't pass up the chance to tease his daughter.

"Yeah. He has an auto detailing shop. I'm guessing since you didn't know that, and from all those marks on your neck, you two didn't do too much talking last night."

She gasped, covering her mouth, and avoiding her father's eyes.

"I gotta go, Daddy. I'll be back in a few hours."

She hightailed it out of the door so fast, she forgot to grab the keys to her mother's car. When she came back in, her father had them in his hand. She reached for them, and he snatched his hand away.

"You don't need to be embarrassed, baby girl." He chuckled. "The way you were smiling when you walked out of your room did my heart good. You haven't smiled like that in years."

He handed her the keys, and she turned around and left without a word. No matter how grown she was, Everleigh refused to talk to her daddy about sex.

CHAPTER 10

By the time Everleigh arrived at MAAD, Myles had finished detailing his first car of the day. He had one more waiting that he would do after lunch. Since there was nowhere for them to sit and eat at his place of business, he decided they could go to a deli that was a few buildings over.

"Hey, baby," he greeted Everleigh.

She was standing at the front counter when he walked out of the bathroom. His dick noticed how good her ass was looking in the jeans she was wearing. When she turned to face him, her smile was as wide as his.

"Is this your business?"

He kissed her lips before replying. "It is."

"Oh my God, Myles. Why didn't you tell me?"

He shrugged his shoulders. "We had more important stuff to deal with."

"What about last night?"

"I had more important stuff to deal with, like reclaiming my pussy. Let's go."

She giggled and shook her head at his forwardness. He'd always been that way, and she was glad that he hadn't changed. After locking up, he took her hand, and they walked in the direction of the deli.

"Where are we going?" she asked.

"Just a few buildings over to this lil deli. As you saw, ain't much room at my spot, so I eat there a lot. The food is good."

"I remember how much you like deli sandwiches."

"I'm not hard to please. Just give me a—"

"Croissant sandwich with turkey, provolone cheese, honey mustard, one tomato slice, and a few sliced sweet pickles," Everleigh proudly recited.

Myles couldn't hide the grin on his face. After so many years, she remembered his favorite sandwich. He kissed her temple as they continued to walk.

"You really do love a nigga, huh?"

"I never stopped."

They walked in silence for a minute before Everleigh spoke again.

"My dad said he saw you this morning."

"Yeah, we chopped it up for a few minutes before I left."

"He saw all these hickies you left on my neck. Why did you mark me up like this?"

She lifted her neck and turned her head in different directions so he could see all the marks he left.

"Damn, baby. I ain't know I gotchu like that. That phenomenal ass shit between your legs almost had me screamin' like a bitch. I used your neck to stifle myself. My bad."

He stopped in the middle of the sidewalk and buried his head in her neck. When she felt his tongue graze her skin, tingles flowed through her body. He then began to suck, and it took her a few seconds but she pushed him away.

"How you gon' apologize but then try to leave another mark? I'm glad I don't have anywhere important to be. I'd have to use a pound of makeup to hide these things."

He gave her a smirk as they continued walking. Less than five minutes later, they were entering the deli. It was a small but nice-looking establishment. When they found a booth, Everleigh sat down, while Myles remained standing. She looked around to see if something was wrong but didn't see anything strange.

"Are you gonna sit down?"

"Yeah, when you scoot your ass over," he replied.

Everleigh looked at him like he was crazy, but just as she was about to snap back, she remembered. When they were dating, Myles never sat across from her in a booth, always on the same side. She felt kind of bad for forgetting, and she thought that might be why his tone was a little off. She moved over, and he slid in next to her.

Once he was seated, he picked up two menus and gave one to her. As he looked through it, Everleigh stared at the side of his face, waiting for him to look at her.

"Are you seriously mad I didn't remember?" she asked.

He didn't respond, so she continued.

"Just a few minutes ago, you were singing my praises when I remembered your favorite sandwich. Now you mad 'cause I—"

"I remember everything about you," he said, keeping his eyes on the menu.

"I'm sure you forgot something. It's been years, and you probably ran through a slew of women since then."

"I sure did, but all them bitches were forgettable. They weren't you, Leigh."

"Aww, I'm sorry, baby. I didn't *forget* forget. It just slipped my mind for a second."

She angled her body towards his and put her arms around his neck, then planted kisses all over the side of his face.

"Don't be mad, Myles. I'll make it up to you later."

He turned his face toward hers and smiled. They were so close their noses were almost touching.

"How?"

"However you want."

He pulled his head back a little bit and raised one of his eyebrows.

"You sure 'bout that? Because—"

"I'm positive."

She pulled his head back toward hers and their lips met. Everleigh pushed her tongue between Myles's lips, and they shared a passionate kiss until they were interrupted by someone clearing their throat. They separated and looked in the direction of the disruption.

"I'm sorry. I was just wondering if I could get you something to drink."

Everleigh wiped her lip gloss from Myles's lips and faced forward, before picking up the menu.

"Two lemonades and two waters," Myles told the young waiter.

"Okay. I'll be right back with those."

He walked away, and Myles put his arm around her shoulders.

"You see how I remembered you like lemonade."

Although he couldn't see her eyes, she rolled them. "Boy, everybody likes lemonade. I'm not impressed.

"I'm just sayin'."

They looked through the menu, and when the waiter returned, they placed their order. As they waited for their food, Myles rubbed Everleigh's thigh. He was getting dangerously close to her center, and her panties had become moist. He was the only man that could make her pussy wet from doing next to nothing. He noticed her squirming in her seat and stopped rubbing for a second, then squeezed her thigh.

"What's wrong, Leigh?" he said with a smirk, knowing damn well she was getting turned on.

"Nothing, but don't get mad if I start rubbing your dick under this table."

He chuckled. "Why would I get mad? I welcome that shit. Give me your hand."

"Oh my God, Myles. I'm not about to stroke your dick in here. People can see everything we're doing under this table. Those women over there already been staring since we sat down."

He looked in the direction that she leaned her head, and when he spotted the women, Everleigh noticed an expression of recognition before he frowned.

"Why are you frowning?"

"Because I used to fuck 'em both, and I ain't even know they knew each other."

Everleigh kissed her teeth and pushed him away from her. He shrugged his shoulders and took a sip of his lemonade as if he'd said nothing of importance. Minutes later, the waiter came back with their lunch, and Myles said a quick prayer before they began to eat. Since they hadn't had a chance to really talk since their reunion, they took that time to update each other on the past twelve years. Myles couldn't be as open with her as she was with him, considering what his lifestyle consisted of, but he was excited to tell her about the last few years.

"I can't believe you finally went back to school. I'm so proud of you."

"It's just an associate degree. I had to learn a lil somethin' about runnin' a legitimate business before I started one."

"All I have is an associate degree, too. Don't downplay your accomplishment, baby. Did you have a party to celebrate?"

"Hell, naw. I ain't even go to graduation. I just had them send me my shit in the mail." He took another sip of his lemonade. "What about you, Miss Celebrity Photographer? Who was your first famous client?"

"Oh my God. Would you believe it was MC Lyte?"

"No shit?"

She nodded with a huge smile as she thought about the beginning of her career. Photography was the only thing that made her happy back then because she was sick over her breakup with Myles.

"Damn, baby. You was doing it big out the gate."

"It was crazy how it happened. I was shadowing a well-established and well-known photographer, and he got sick. I think it was food poisoning or something. Anyway, I had to fill in, and she loved my work so much, she started booking me for everything and referred me to others."

"That's cool as hell. I'm proud of you." He leaned in her direction, and they shared a quick kiss.

Although they had jealous eyes on them the whole time, they managed to enjoy their meal, as they played catch-up and even did a little reminiscing.

CHAPTER 11

Over the next couple of weeks, Everleigh and Myles both had some loose ends they needed to tie up. Everleigh spent a little time adjusting her photography calendar. Some photo shoots were coming up that she needed to reschedule and some that she had to find another photographer for. Thankfully, all of her clients were very understanding. The rest of her time was split between her father and Myles.

Everette was still sleeping in the recliner, and she wasn't sure when he'd be ready to go back to the bedroom. She didn't push him, but she was a little concerned about his mental state, along with his comfort. A couple of days ago, he agreed to go to grief therapy, and Everleigh offered to go with him. The first session was later that day, and she was hopeful.

Although Everette had accepted his wife's death, he was having a hard time figuring out how to move forward without her. They had been retired for years and spent almost all of their time together. It was hard for him not having her there. A few of his friends had stopped by, and he enjoyed talking with them, but he missed his wife.

Everette enjoyed having Everleigh home and was happy that she was no longer engaged to Easton. She and Myles spent a lot of time with him, which he appreciated, and he was pleased to see that the love between them was as strong as it had ever been, maybe even stronger.

Myles had been avoiding talking to Nyema. She'd been calling or texting him a few times a day for the past several days. They didn't have the type of relationship where they talked or saw each other every day, but she expected to see him at least once a week. He knew if he didn't reach out soon, she'd pop up at his shop. She wouldn't dare go to his house without an invitation.

After having breakfast with Everleigh, he dropped her back off at her father's house and went to work. Today, he had a minivan and an SUV to detail, which would take about five or six hours each. However, he was determined to end things officially with Nyema. He didn't feel like he owed that courtesy to the other women he fucked off with. He just blocked their numbers and left it at that. So, before he got started on the first car, he called Nyema.

"Hey, baby," she greeted. "You've been hard to catch up with."

"Yeah, I've been kinda busy."

"Well, I'm glad you finally made the time to call me back. I miss you."

She wasn't making it easy.

"Aye, you busy around one? I can come up to the mall."

Nyema worked as a registered nurse at UW Medical Center.

"I'm working three to three, so I can meet you there before I go in."

"Cool, I'll meet you in the food court," he told her.

"Okay."

He ended the call and blew out a breath. Nyema hadn't ever given him any problems about how he moved. She knew she wasn't the only woman in his life, but Myles wasn't sure how she would handle him ending their situationship. All he could do was hope for the best.

A few hours later, he heard his phone vibrating on one of the counters in the garage. When he reached it, a smile graced his face when he saw the picture on the screen.

"Hey, beautiful," he answered.

"Hey, baby. I was calling to see if you wanted me to bring you some lunch. I know you said you had a busy day today."

"I appreciate that Leigh, but I'm good. I'm still full from breakfast."

"Okay. Daddy has a therapy session today. If he doesn't need me to stay, I'm gonna go down to Kubota Garden and take some pictures while I wait for him."

"That's cool. I'll see you when I get off. I love you."

"Love you more."

He had another hour to work before he left to meet Nyema. Time flew by, but he was able to finish up the minivan before it was time for him to go. After changing into a dry, clean shirt, he headed to the mall. Nyema sent him a text telling him to meet her near Caliburger.

The closer he got to the food court, his stomach began to growl. He didn't feel hungry until he smelled food. As he approached the tables near the restaurant, he saw Nyema and was surprised that she had her four-year-old daughter, Kai, with her.

Myles had spent time with Nyema and Kai several times, and the little girl had grown on him. He tried not to get too attached to her and hoped she wouldn't get attached, either. However, it happened anyway.

"Myles," Kai sang when he spotted him. She jumped out of the chair she was sitting in and ran to him.

"Hey, Cutie Kai," he responded with the nickname he'd given to her as he leaned down to pick her up.

"I didn't see you for a long time. Mommy said you was real busy."

"Mommy is right. Have you been a good girl?"

"Mmmhmm," she said while nodding.

When they made it to the table, Myles put Kai back in her seat and sat across from Nyema. Seeing him interact with her daughter made Nyema very happy, and she had a huge smile on her face.

"I didn't know you were bringing Kai. We could have rescheduled," he told Nyema.

"I didn't plan on it. She starts camp next week, and my sister has been watching her. Something important came up, and I'm taking her to her father's on my way to work. I didn't think you'd mind since you haven't seen her in a while."

"It's always good to see Cutie Kai." He tapped her nose with his index finger when she looked up at him. "But I kinda wanted to talk to you...privately."

"Oh, okay. Let me order her food, and she can listen to her headphones while she eats."

As Nyema stood, Myles took some cash out of his pocket and handed it to her.

"Get something for yourself, too. I'm good."

Nyema walked away, feeling a little nervous about what Myles wanted to discuss. She no longer had an appetite, but she ordered something for herself anyway. When she returned to the table, Myles had Kai giggling uncontrollably about something.

"What's so funny over here?" she asked.

"Mommy, Myles said Clayton can't be my boyfriend 'cause I can't have a boyfriend until I'm a hundred years old." She continued to giggle as if that was the funniest thing in the world.

"Maybe not a hundred years old, baby, but you need to be much older than four," Nyema explained to her daughter.

After giving Kai her food, headphones, and iPad, she looked at Myles expectantly.

"What'd you want to talk about?" she asked before taking a bite of her sandwich.

"Look, I'm not gon' beat around the bush because there's no easy way to say this. A couple weeks ago, I reconnected with my ex, and we got back together. I can't see you anymore."

Nyema repeatedly blinked while shaking her head.

"What? Your ex—you—who is your ex? We've been seeing each other for years and—"

"We were never exclusive, Ny, but I respect you enough to end things the right way."

A few tears fell from her eyes as she tried to calm herself.

"The right way. This is what you call the right way, huh? You strung me along all these years…had me thinking we could actually be something."

"Come on, Ny. I never led you or any other woman on. If you made some shit up in your head about what we were or what we coulda been, that's on you. I made it clear that I didn't want a serious relationship with you."

"Yeah, that's what you said, but your actions—"

"My actions, what? We never kissed, I ain't never ate your pussy, and we ain't never stayed the night at each other's house. What did my actions say, Nyema?"

She took a deep breath and gathered herself. She had no one to blame but herself because Myles never promised forever. He never promised her anything but outstanding dick.

"You're right, Myles. I appreciate you coming to me like a man and letting me know that you're moving on. Can you, umm, leave now? I, uhh, I need a minute to get myself together."

A part of Myles wanted to apologize, but for what? She knew not to catch feelings. Instead, he looked down at Kai, who was enjoying her food and whatever was playing on her iPad screen. He reached over and pulled one of her headphones off her ear.

"Cutie Kai, I gotta go, okay? I probably won't see you for a long time, so here's some money to buy yourself some ice cream for the rest of the summer."

"Yayyyy," she cheered as she took the bills from him. "Thank you, Myles. Why I'm not gonna see you? You gonna be real busy again?"

"Yep, I'm gonna be real busy, but if I see you out with Clayton, I might have to chase him away."

"Nooo, you can't 'cause he's my boyfriend."

"No more of that boyfriend stuff."

He picked her up and tickled her until she was in a laughing fit, making Nyema feel even worse. It saddened her that things between them were over. He kissed Kai's forehead before returning her to her seat and standing. He knew Nyema was trying to avoid his eyes, but he slid his index finger under her chin and lifted her head.

"It wasn't my intent to hurt you, Ny." He leaned down and kissed her forehead as he did her daughters. "You be good."

When he walked away, Nyema was on the verge of a breakdown. She always wondered why he was so closed off and wouldn't even entertain the idea of a committed relationship with her. Myles enjoyed her company, but his heart belonged to Everleigh. Now that she was back in his life, he refused to let anything come between them.

CHAPTER 12

After Everleigh dropped her father off at his therapy session, it began to rain. She decided to go to the mall for an hour and a half since Kubota Garden was now out of the question because of the rain. She actually needed to buy a few things because her wardrobe was a little light. In her rush to get to her mother, she didn't pack very much, and she didn't leave many things at her parents' house the last time she was home.

Everleigh wasn't the kind of woman that enjoyed shopping, so after buying a few pairs of shorts and shirts and a couple of sundresses, she was on her way to the food court. Her mind was on a Calibello Mushroom Burger and a strawberry shake from CaliBurger. She'd been craving both since the last time she was home.

As she approached the restaurant, she thought she saw someone that looked like Myles. The man was sitting with a woman and little girl, so she knew it wasn't him, but her feet moved a little faster to get a closer look, just to be sure. The closer she got, the more confused she became. Her feet stopped moving when her eyes confirmed that it was definitely Myles.

She watched as he tickled a little girl, who was laughing hysterically before he kissed her on her forehead and put her in the seat next to him. All Myles had to do was look up, and he'd see Everleigh, but he was focused on dealing with the situation in front of him. He said a few words to the woman at the table, kissed her forehead, and unknowingly walked in Everleigh's direction.

He was in deep thought and wasn't paying much attention to his surroundings, which wasn't like him. Before he realized it, the woman he loved was standing before him, with hurt and anger all over her face.

"Baby, what are you doing here?" he asked, obviously surprised to see her.

"What am *I* doing here? What the fuck are you doing here? And who the hell is that woman and child?".

Everleigh's voice was slightly elevated, causing Myles to look around. A few people were looking in their direction, so he took the bags she was holding from her hands and headed to the door where he entered.

"You gon' just ignore my questions? And I don't need you to carry my bags."

She tried to grab them from him, but he lifted them out of her reach and kept walking.

"I'm not ignoring you. I'm just not tryin' to talk to you about this shit here. If you want some answers, bring your ass on."

Everleigh stopped walking and folded her arms across her chest. Myles didn't notice that she wasn't behind him until he was several feet away. When he turned and saw her stance, he groaned because she was being difficult.

"Leigh, baby, I promise, whatever you thinkin', it ain't it. Come with me so I can explain this shit to you."

"How about I just go ask her who she is to you? Maybe I'll get some answers *right* fuckin' now."

She turned around and was on her way back to the food court, and Myles dropped her bags where he stood to go after her. She didn't get very far before he snatched her up as discreetly as he could and put his mouth close to her ear.

"Leigh, stop fuckin' playin' with me and bring your ass on. Whatever the fuck you thinkin', wipe that shit outta your mind. Now, let's go," he whispered, but with bass in his voice, then walked away.

All this time, Everleigh thought her and her pussy were on the same team. However, while her mind was still trying to be mad at Myles, her pussy was like, *"Bitch, why you still standing here? You better go after that dick!"*

Myles was damn near out the door by the time she caught up with him. When she got outside, she realized that she came in through a different entrance. She stopped walking again, and Myles turned around, releasing a deep breath.

"Fuck, Leigh! It's raining, and I ain't about to keep going back and forth. You comin' or not?"

"My car is parked at another entrance."

"I'll drive you to your car when we finish talking. Wait here and come out when I pull up. I'll be right back."

He put her bags down beside her, exited the doors, and jogged to his truck. When he pulled up, she went outside, and he was waiting with the passenger door open. He took her bags and helped her inside, before putting them in the trunk.

"Where you parked?" he asked once he was in his truck.

"By P.F. Chang's," she replied with an attitude.

Gripping the steering wheel, Myles shook his head. "I got something big to adjust that lil attitude you got over there."

"Whatever, nigga. You lied to me."

"Ain't nobody lie to your ass, Leigh."

"You said you were full from lunch and—"

"I said I ain't lie to you. I met up with her to let her know we had to stop fuckin' around."

"Wait? You had a girlfriend all this time? How—"

"I ain't said shit about her being my girlfriend. The only woman that ever got that title is you."

"If she was just somebody you were fuckin', why you have to have a special meeting to end it, Myles? And since when did people start bringing kids into those types of situations? Or is that your daughter?"

"You really think I'm the type of nigga that would hide my kid from you? That's fucked up."

She felt a little twinge in her stomach before she replied with, "I was just asking a question. If the kid ain't yours, it was clear that she knew you well."

"I said what I said, Leigh. The kid ain't mine, and I was just fuckin' her mama. You can believe it or not, but ain't shit else for me to say about the situation. Where's your car?"

"Halfway down the next row," she told him, holding on to her attitude.

"I don't know why you mad, anyway. Even if she was my girl-friend, which she wasn't, you had a whole damn fiancé. The hell you gon' be mad at a nigga for movin' on with his life when you the one that left and moved the fuck on with yours?"

Everleigh's mouth opened and closed a few times. She had no response because Myles was absolutely right.

"Why didn't you just tell me you were meeting with her? It makes it seem like you had something to hide."

"You right, it does, and I'm sorry about that. I promise you I ain't got nothin' to hide. Nyema was not my girlfriend, and that's the truth, but she was consistent pussy. I ain't wanna just block her number like I did the others because I got more respect for her than them. Can we be done with this conversation?"

She nodded but was still pouting.

"Fix your damn face, Leigh. Why you poutin' and shit? You don't see me 'round here poutin' 'cause you agreed to marry a nigga that wasn't me."

It was unfair for her to be upset when she had been engaged to be married to another man. As much as Myles wanted to act like it didn't bother him, he was hurt that Everleigh considered marrying someone else. For the time that they were separated, he didn't even consider getting into a serious relationship, let alone marriage. It wouldn't have been fair to him or the other woman, and he knew it. He would have rather spent his life alone than committing to a woman he didn't love.

"I'm, uhh, I—"

"I'll see you when I'm done at the shop," he cut her off.

"I...okay."

Leaning across the console, she kissed his cheek. When she turned to grab the door handle, he touched her thigh, causing her to look at him.

"Don't let shit that don't matter make you doubt how much I love your ass...how much I've always loved you."

Myles grabbed the back of her neck and pulled her face toward his. Their lips collided, and their tongues met soon after. Everleigh's panties were already damp from the way he handled her in the mall. Now, they were becoming soaked from the way his tongue caressed hers with each rotation. She moaned into his mouth, and her whole body was mad when he pulled away. Myles chuckled at the expression on her face.

"I'll take care of that pussy later," he promised.

They shared one last peck before he got out and walked around to help her out of his truck and into her car. She was almost giddy with anticipation for what he would do to her body later that night.

CHAPTER 13

A little over a month had passed since he'd lost his wife, and Everette had been going to therapy twice a week for a couple of weeks. He wasn't ready to sleep in the bedroom yet, but he asked Everleigh to help him start going through her mother's things. She was shocked at his request, but it was then that she knew that therapy was helping. They began early one morning and worked until late afternoon, only taking a couple of breaks. By the time they called it a day, they had quite a few boxes packed up and decided that what they didn't want to keep would be donated to a charity. It was an extremely emotional experience for both of them, but it was also very therapeutic. A lot of laughing and crying occurred, but they managed to get through it.

"Your mom was so proud of you," Everette told his daughter out of the blue. "I'm sure she told you that often."

"She did. You both have always been my biggest cheerleaders."

"You know, when you up and decided to move to L.A., she was a mess. She cried every day for a good month."

"What? I thought she wanted me to go. When I mentioned the job to her, she encouraged me to apply."

"Of course, she did, baby girl. She wanted you to pursue your dreams; we both did. Neither of us were able to do so. When we met, we talked about going to Africa to teach after we earned our teaching degrees. Times were a bit different then, though. Teachers complain about their salaries now, but when we started," he shook his head. "We made next to nothing."

"Wow! I never knew that was something you wanted to do. That would have been amazing."

"It sure would have. By the time we were established enough to afford something like that, you came along. Once you were born, you were our main focus. We tried for so long and suffered so many losses to have you, but you were worth every one of them. God couldn't have blessed us with a better daughter."

Everleigh was now in tears. She always knew that she was spoiled, and there was never a time when she didn't feel how much her parents loved her.

"God couldn't have blessed me with better parents. I've always known that I was blessed, and I love and appreciate you and Ma for all you've instilled in me. It means more than anything material that you've ever given me."

The two of them sat in an embrace for an extended amount of time before Everette pulled away and spoke again.

"Are you and Myles planning a future together? Or is this temporary until you go back to L.A.?"

"We haven't talked about the future."

"Well, I'm not gonna pry. I'm sure you'll figure it out."

"We probably should talk about it. I've just been enjoying getting to know him again. It's kinda weird because I feel like he's changed so much, but yet, he's still the same man I fell in love with."

"Is that good or bad, baby girl?"

"It's perfect. It's like, this is the man I knew he could be back then. I guess it just took him some time to..."

"Mature?"

"Yeah, mature, I guess."

"I hate the circumstances that brought you back together, but I'm happy that you two reunited. I've always believed he was the one for you. I want you with a man that loves you like I loved—like I still love, your mother. I believe Myles is that man."

"Me too, Daddy."

⚜

ONE THE OTHER SIDE OF TOWN, MYLES WAS THINKING ABOUT having some alone time with his lady. He had been spending most nights at the Noble residence, only sleeping at his place a couple times a week. Although Everleigh had been there a few times, she had yet to stay over. Myles was itching to have her all to himself for a full night. After he finished detailing the last car for the day, he sent her a text.

Me: Hey beautiful
Mine: Hey you done for the day?
Me: Just finished. Wanted to ask you something.
Mine: Ok
Me: How you feel about staying at my place?
Mine: Tonight?
Me: Yeah

The three dots appeared then disappeared a few times before his phone rang with a call from Everleigh.

"Wassup?"

"Hey, baby. Umm, I don't know. You think my dad will be okay?"

"Just talk to him and see how he feels about it. Shit, I'm sure he's sick of the sound of us fuckin'."

She and Myles had made love every night since they'd been reunited, except for the first few days of her period. After the third day, he seduced her in the shower each morning before her cycle ended. Even on the days he slept at his house, he managed to get his dick wet between her thighs before they went their separate ways for the night.

"Oh my God, Myles. You said you didn't think he could hear us."

"Damn, baby, you be loud sometimes. I'm sure he's heard you a few times."

"That is so embarrassing."

"We grown, Leigh. It ain't that serious."

"Would you want Ms. Delilah to hear you having sex?"

"I mean, I'd rather she not, but if she do, ain't no shame in my game," he replied, shrugging his shoulders.

"Typical male answer. I'll talk to him and call you back. Love you."

"Love you more."

After ending the call, Myles straightened up the shop and prepped everything for the following day, then locked up. Before heading home, he stopped at Trader Joe's to pick up a bottle of chardonnay, Everleigh's favorite kind of wine. He wasn't a wine drinker and didn't realize how many different brands of chardonnay there were. Before becoming too frustrated, he grabbed a bottle of Cocobon Roasted Oak Chardonnay and hoped it was one that she liked. Just as he pulled into his driveway, she called and said she'd be there in about an hour, which gave Myles enough time to shower and order some food.

As he finished his shower, he heard his phone vibrating on the bathroom counter. He was gonna ignore the call until he saw that it was his sister, Myla.

"Wassup, baby sis."

"I don't know, you tell me. Since Everleigh's been back in town, me and Mommy haven't heard from you much."

"That's probably true."

"It's definitely true. I miss you."

"My, how the hell you got time to miss anybody with a husband, two badass toddlers, and a spoiled ass infant?"

"First of all, my kids are not bad or spoiled. I can't believe you over there talking about your nieces and nephew like that."

Right on cue, one of Myla's kids started cutting up in the background.

"You sure 'bout that?"

"Oh my God! KJ, put that down and get off your sister's back. Myles, I'll call you back."

She ended the call before Myles could say he told her so. He laughed at her, but deep down, he couldn't wait for that to be his life.

A little over an hour later, Everleigh was ringing his doorbell. When he opened the door, his eyes roamed over her body. She was wearing a simple, short, fitted, yellow T-shirt dress with a pair of yellow Converse. Her thick hair was in a puff on the top of her head, and her face was free of makeup. To Myles, she'd never looked more beautiful.

"Umm, are you gonna let me in or stare at me all night?" she asked after a few long seconds.

"What if I said I wanna stare at you all night?"

"I'd say if you let me in, I could take these clothes off, and you could stare at a naked me."

"Aww, shit. Bring your fine ass in here."

He pulled her inside and into his arms, against his naked chest. She dropped her overnight bag on the floor and wrapped her arms around his neck as his hands went to her ass. You would have thought they hadn't seen each other this morning, the way they were going at it. Just as he was about to lift her up and guide her legs around his waist, someone cleared their throat. When that didn't get their attention, the person spoke.

"Excuse me. I have a delivery for Myles Abbott."

They finally separated, and Myles rudely snatched the food and closed the door in the man's face.

"Myles, that was so rude."

"What? I already gave him a generous tip. What I gotta be nice for?"

Instead of replying, she just shook her head.

"You wanna eat dinner now? Or can I eat your pussy first?"

"I swear your ass is so nasty. I need you to feed me before I feed you."

He chuckled. "I guess that's fair."

After slipping her shoes off, Everleigh followed Myles to his kitchen, where she sat at the table while he put the food on the counter and washed his hands.

"What'd you get? Smells like Italian."

"It's a pan of baked lasagna from Buca di Beppo. I figured what we don't eat, I can take for lunch or have leftovers."

"It smells so good. Did you get garlic bread?"

"Regular and mozzarella."

She watched as he prepared their plates. When he finished, he brought them over to the table, then asked if she wanted lemonade or her favorite wine.

"You remembered my favorite wine?"

"I remembered you like chardonnay. Have your taste buds changed?"

"Not at all. I'll have wine."

She planned to get real loose tonight, so wine was the perfect thing to assist with that. He poured her a glass, then got a beer for himself, before taking the seat next to her. They held hands while he blessed the food, then proceeded to dig in.

"How was your day?" he asked after swallowing his first bite.

"It was good. My dad decided he was ready to go through some of my ma's things."

"Oh, shit. How'd that go?"

"Surprisingly well. We laughed as much as we cried, so I think that's good."

He enjoyed a few bites of his food before he responded.

"That's real good. I'm surprised he's ready so soon. Therapy must be pretty good for him."

"I think so. He also asked about us."

"What about us?"

Everleigh was a little hesitant to answer him. It was no question that she wanted a future with Myles, and he'd let her know that he wouldn't let her walk out of his life again. However, no definite plans had been made.

"You gon' answer me?" he said when she didn't respond.

"He asked if we were planning a future together or if this is temporary."

"What'd you tell him?"

"That we hadn't talked about it because we haven't. At least not in great detail."

Myles gulped the last of his beer and leaned back in the chair, while Everleigh slowly lifted the fork to her mouth.

"I thought I'd made myself clear, but apparently not. So, I'm gonna tell you like I told you a few weeks ago. You're mine, Leigh. I let you walk out of my life once already, but that shit won't happen again. I realize you have a life in L.A., and we got some shit to figure out, but we gon' figure it out together."

She couldn't hide her smile as she put her fork down and stood from her seat to straddle his lap. As they sat face to face, Everleigh rested her arms on his shoulders, and she softly kissed his lips.

"You done eating? 'Cause you can't be puttin' that hot pussy on me like this unless you wanna start some shit."

"I'm done eating. I thought you might be ready for your dessert."

"I been ready, baby."

Their lips connected again, but this time there was nothing soft about the kiss. This time, it was fierce and passionate. Myles loved making love to Everleigh, and kissing her was a *very* close second. He didn't know if it was because it was something he didn't partake in for over a decade, or if it was because it was Everleigh. He had a feeling it was the latter.

She could feel his dick poking at the crotch of her panties, so she began to wind her hips, creating friction that felt so good. Wrapping her legs around the back legs of the chair, she used the leverage and pulled her middle as close as she could to his.

"Mmm," she moaned.

Suddenly, Myles smacked her ass, surprising her, causing her to loosen her legs from around the chair. Tightening the grip he had on her ass, he stood and walked them to the breakfast bar. After sitting Everleigh on top, he gently pushed her so that she was lying on her back, then reached under her T-shirt dress and ripped her panties off. Lifting her legs to his shoulders, he buried his face between her thighs and destroyed her pussy with his tongue.

"Oh, shiitttt!" she screamed.

Since they'd been back together, Myles had eaten her pussy multiple times. However, he took it up a notch because he wanted to hear her scream at the top of her lungs. For that reason, his tongue showed no mercy.

"Oh—my—God, baby! Myles—fuckkkkk!"

The louder she screamed, the harder he went. When her hands went to the top of his head, and she clamped her legs around his neck, he knew her climax was on the brink. That was just the motivation he needed to shift the speed of his tongue into the next gear. Within seconds, she was screaming his name as her juices sprayed all over his face.

"Ahhh, my damn! Oh shit! Please, baby, wait! Mmm, don't stop!" Everleigh rambled.

Because she was on the breakfast bar, she couldn't run because she would have gone headfirst to the floor on the other side. Myles took advantage of that and devoured her pussy until she reached a second climax and was begging him to stop.

When he stood to his full height again, he caught her legs as they fell from his shoulders. Everleigh's breathing was extremely labored as she tried to catch her breath. Myles picked her up bridal style and carried her to his bedroom. Once he placed her on the bed, he lifted off her dress and reached behind her to unsnap her bra.

As Myles stood in front of her, she could see his dick print through the basketball shorts he was wearing, and the tip peeking from the waistband. Her mouth became moist, and she licked her lips. He noticed how she was staring, and a smirk graced his face. Grabbing the waistband of his shorts, he slowly pushed them down, and his erection sprang free.

After stepping out of his shorts, Everleigh reached for his manhood, gripping the base before slowly licking the fluid the was leaking from the head.

"Ssss," Myles hissed when his dick and her tongue made contact.

She teased him by twirling her tongue around the tip several times before taking as much of him as she could in her mouth. What her mouth didn't cover, her hand did, and they moved in sync as she bobbed her head. With the perfection suction and pace, Everleigh worked her magic to pull his nut out.

"Got damn, baby!"

His hands went to either side of her head to control her movements. Instead of resisting, she let him guide the tempo but used her tongue and jaws to get the results she desired. The pulsing began, slowly at first, then Myles tried to stifle a moan, unsuccessfully.

"Mmm, shit!" he slipped from his lips, followed by, "Fuucckk, baby!"

With no warning, he shot his seeds down her throat, and she willingly swallowed every drop. When she kept sucking, Myles released a deep growl and pushed her away, causing her to fall back on the bed, as she laughed at his reaction.

"You tryna kill me or some shit?" he said, obviously out of breath.

"Please, baby. You do the same thing to me. I'm just not strong enough to push you away."

"Yeah, okay. Spread them legs and let me see you play with that pussy."

She did what he said, opening her legs wide and pushing two of her fingers inside. His dick responded immediately, so he didn't let her pleasure herself for long.

"Damn, Leigh. You makin' me jealous, baby," he told her as he crawled between her legs.

Pulling her fingers from her haven, she lifted them to Myles's mouth, and he licked her juices away. After savoring her flavor for the second time that evening, his hands cupped her breasts, and he took one of her nipples in his mouth. His tongue circled her chocolate areola before he sucked it into his mouth, then did the same to the other. When his dick tapped her entrance, he went ahead and pushed into her eager womb, then buried his face into her neck.

"Mmm," she moaned as her walls adjusted to his size.

She wrapped her legs around his thighs and gripped his ass, urging him to go deeper, and with each thrust, he did precisely that.

Lifting his head, he looked into her eyes, as he went deeper and deeper, and asked, "You gon' be my wife and give me some babies, Leigh?"

As her climax began to build, Everleigh closed her eyes and got lost in pleasure. She heard him and wanted to give him an answer, but her focus was on the sensational feeling he was delivering between her thighs. Right when she was about to reach her peak, Myles stopped moving, and her eyes popped open.

"I asked you a question."

"Yes, baby, yes. I'll marry you and have your babies. Now please, make me cum."

Getting on his knees, he propped Everleigh's legs on his shoulders, then proceeded to plummet her pussy. Every pound elicited loud, sensual, satisfied moans from her.

"You ready to cum?" he whispered.

"Oh God, yes!"

In this position, she could feel every inch of him, and she would bet her last dollar that his dick was rearranging vital organs. As her orgasm neared, she felt the familiar tingles all over her body, before it began to convulse. What made it even better was the pulsing of his dick, combined with the throbbing of her pussy. Together, they reached the highest point of ecstasy, before collapsing in each other's arms.

CHAPTER 14

I t was time. It was actually past time. Close to six weeks had gone by, and Everleigh had yet to return her L.A. She'd been declining all of Easton's calls and ignoring his text messages. However, she knew that wasn't the mature way to deal with their situation. They had a whole life together, which included a condo, that was in both their names, where all of her belongings were still housed. She couldn't ignore him forever and honestly, didn't want to end things without proper closure.

The management team of an up and coming artist hand contacted Everleigh to schedule a photo shoot at the last minute. She planned to see if another photographer was interested, but after talking to her father and Myles, she decided to hop on a flight. There were several things that she needed to handle while in L.A., one of them being her relationship with Easton.

Layne and Robbie were picking her up from the airport, and she would be staying with one of them while she was in town. Myles let her know that staying at the condo she once shared with Easton was out of the question. As soon as she hopped in the backseat of Layne's car at the airport, she and Robbie turned around, gave her a once over, then looked at each other knowingly.

"Yep! You were right," Robbie said.

"I told you. Now, give me my fifty dollars," Layne demanded, holding out her hand

"Y'all two heffas making bets on me? The hell!"

"It was just a little wager to see if you would be still sportin' that well-fucked glow. You shinin' so bright we need to wear our shades to look at your ass," Robbie confessed.

"What kinda sperm that nigga got? 'Cause damn! You're skin always been clear, but your shit is next level now," Layne added.

"You know what? Y'all are certifiable. Drop me off at the nearest hotel."

"Not a chance. We took some days off just for you. Now, where are we going first?"

Layne worked as a paralegal for some big law firm in downtown L.A. and Robbie owned two flower shops, one in Santa Monica and one in Hollywood.

"I'm starving, so let's go eat," Everleigh suggested.

Traffic in the city of Los Angeles was pure torture, but since Everleigh's condo was downtown and they'd be headed there, after they ate, they braved the traffic to get to their favorite burger joint. They ordered their food at the counter and was lucky enough to find a tiny booth available in the back. Layne went to save the booth, while Everleigh and Robbie headed over to the drink dispenser and got their drinks. Minutes later, their food arrived.

"Have you heard from Easton?" Layne asked.

"I have, but I've been ignoring him. Honestly, I've been enjoying reconnecting with Myles and didn't want Easton to fuck up my vibe."

"I feel that," Robbie agreed. "But what exactly is your plan. Are you moving back to Seattle?"

"My heart is telling me that's where I need to be. Daddy's having a hard time dealing with Ma being gone. I miss the hell outta her, too, but can you imagine being with someone for over fifty years and then, boom, just like that, they're gone?"

"I can't imagine what he's going through. My parents never married, but were pretty good friends, so when my mom died, my dad was sad but nothing to the extent that I'm sure your dad is experiencing," Layne said.

"I'm sure it'll be like that with my parents. They've been together since they were in their twenties," Robbie added. "I would understand if you decided to move back."

"He started grief therapy a few weeks ago, and I think it's helping, but I don't know when or if I'll ever feel comfortable being away from him for an extended amount of time again."

"And then there's Myles," Layne cooed.

Everleigh's smile was as bright as the sun when she thought of Myles. How she felt with Easton versus how she felt with Myles was like night and day. She hadn't realized how much she was settling when it came to her happiness while with Easton.

"Yes...and then there's Myles. I wish I could relay to y'all how in love with this man I was...well, I am, but I'm talking about before we broke up."

"Why'd y'all break up again?" Robbie asked. "You never did say."

"It was complicated, and neither of us wanted to break up. It just had to be done."

Although Robbie and Layne had become her best friends, she thought it best not to share the details of Myles's previous life.

"Clearly, it's not something you want to talk about because you've avoided sharing both times it was brought up. I feel you, girl. Let those horrible memories stay buried and make some new ones," Layne told her.

"I plan to. Being in his presence again, even with the planning of my mother's funeral, has been...I can't even explain it. It's like he's what I've been missing."

"Shit, sounds to me like there's not much to decide. You need to start packing, sis!" Layne exclaimed.

"Myles wants to get married," she blurted out.

"He proposed?" they said simultaneously.

"No, not exactly." She smiled as she thought about his request while his dick was buried deep inside of her. "But he let me know his intentions."

"Man, this is some Lifetime movie shit. Don't you know some

producers? Forget Lifetime, this needs to be on the big screen," Robbie said.

"I don't know about all that, but I'm excited about the future for the first time in a long time."

"What about your studio?" Robbie asked.

Everleigh had been leasing a space that she used as her studio, Shots by E, for about five years.

"I still have six or seven months until the lease is up. I'll see if anybody in my photographer circle wants to sublease it. If not, I can probably ride out the lease and travel back and forth for shoots. But enough about me, what's been up with y'all?"

As they finished their meal, Robbie and Layne updated Everleigh on the past few weeks of their lives. When they finished eating, they made their way over to the condo that Everleigh shared with Easton. She planned to fill a few suitcases with as much as she could and meet with him the following day after the photo shoot to discuss how they would move forward. However, when the three of them entered the condo, soft music and moans could be heard coming from the bedroom.

"Y'all hear that?" Everleigh whispered.

They both nodded as the three of them looked toward the bedroom.

"Does it sound like what I think it sounds like?" Everleigh continued to whisper.

"Like somebody getting their back blown out? Sure does," Layne confirmed.

"Are we in the right apartment?" Robbie asked.

"We sure the fuck are, and I know damn well this nigga ain't fuckin' no bitch in my shit."

Everleigh was glad she had on a pair of leggings and running shoes because somebody was about to get their ass kicked. She took long strides to the bedroom and pushed the door open, causing it to hit the doorstop. The two culprits were so lost in the moment, they didn't hear a thing.

Without saying a word, Everleigh ran to the bed, and with one leap, she was behind Easton, who was on his knees, pumping in and out of some woman. Her arm went around his neck, and she squeezed as hard as she could. The woman he was fucking, screamed bloody murder, as she scrambled from underneath him and hopped off the bed. Easton was choking from the pressure of Everleigh's forearm around his neck. By the time he realized what was happening, she had put him on his back, and her knee was in his chest.

"You dirty dick nigga!" she shouted as her fists connected to his face a few times.

"Damn, Ev! Cut it out!" Easton tried to yell, but he was gasping for air.

Finally, he got ahold of Everleigh's wrists, then tossed her to one side of the bed. Hopping out on the other side, he grabbed a pillow to cover up his condom-less dick. But Everleigh wasn't done with his ass. She snatched the lamp off the bedside table and threw it across the bed. Easton ducked just in time and missed getting hit.

"I can't believe you got some bitch in my shit! Nigga are you crazy?" Everleigh continued to shout and throw anything she could get her hands on.

Easton was hit with remotes, shoes, an empty glass, a Bluetooth speaker, and a few other things. Everleigh may have missed him with the lamp, but she hit her target with every other item except the speaker. The whole time this was going on, the blonde barbie he was fucking, was in the corner screaming, while Layne and Robbie stood by the door, laughing hysterically.

"I swear to God, Ev, if you don't cut it out, I'm calling the police," Easton threatened.

He was lucky that she couldn't find anything else to throw at his simple ass.

"Call the police! My name is on this lease, too, you dumbass. You and that pale hoe in the corner will go to jail before I do. "

"Just calm down, please. We can talk this out," he pleaded.

"Ain't shit to talk about! I've been done with your ass. If there was any inkling of hope, which there wasn't, you just fucked that up royally. Now, you got five minutes to get you and that bitch outta my shit. If you take one minute more, I'm calling the police on your bitch-ass."

As Everleigh walked to the bedroom door, she made a quick move toward blonde barbie, like she was about to jump on her. You would have thought she was being beaten to death, the way that woman screamed, causing Layne and Robbie to laugh even louder. Everleigh wasn't in the mood to laugh because she was pissed.

Being petty, she started the timer on her phone, and yelled, "The clock is tickin', nigga. You got four minutes and thirty, twenty-nine, twenty-eight..."

"I can't believe what I just saw. Like, if you told me this shit, I wouldn't believe you," Robbie remarked.

"A white girl, though? For real Easton?" Layne added.

"Man, I don't give a damn who he sticks his weak ass dick in, but for him to bring the bitch here?" She shook her head. "That's a total violation. All my shit is still here, and my name is still on the lease." She looked at her timer then yelled toward the bedroom. "Y'all got three minutes and ten, nine, eight...hurry up, or I swear I'm calling the police."

"Damn, I wish I had thought to take out my phone and record this shit! Y'all could have gone viral," Layne joked.

"Shut your silly ass up!" Robbie said with a laugh.

Everleigh paced back and forth as her friends made jokes. Just as she was about to announce that Easton and blonde barbie had a minute and a half left, they came charging out of the room. While blonde barbie skirted straight for the door, Easton apparently had something he wanted to say, but when opened his mouth to speak, Everleigh held up her hand.

"Nope! Just leave," she told him. "You got thirty seconds, twenty-nine, twenty-eight..."

He shook his head, grabbed his keys off the counter, and left. The condo was dead silent for about twenty seconds when all of a sudden, Everleigh busted out laughing.

"Did y'all see his weak ass stroke game? And ole girl was doing all that damn moaning like that was the best dick she ever had."

"I was expecting to see him digging into her soul, the way she was howling. How the hell did you deal that for three years?" Robbie asked through a laugh.

"I've gone through at least six, maybe eight, vibrators. The motors keep giving out," Everleigh confessed.

"Damn, friend! That's fucked up, and from the looks of it, the nigga is packin'," Layne said, shaking her head. "It's a shame that he got all them inches and don't know how to use 'em."

"A shame it is, but I'm done talking about his ass. Let's start packing."

CHAPTER 15

After packing three large suitcases at Everleigh's condo, they called it a night and headed to Robbie's house in Santa Monica. Later on that night, Everleigh was in one of the guest bedrooms using her phone to check and respond to emails. She wasn't tired, and since it wasn't too late, she called Myles. They'd only spoken once since she landed, and she wanted to hear his voice and see his handsome face.

"Hey, beautiful," Myles answered the FaceTime call.

"Hey. What are you doing?"

"Missin' you. How's it goin'? Get any packing done?"

"I did, but you won't believe what I walked in on." She didn't even wait for him to guess. "Easton was fucking some bitch in my shit!"

"That's fucked up," he replied, but honestly couldn't care less what the next man did with his dick.

"Tell me about it. I was so pissed, I—"

"Why?" he asked, interrupting her.

"Why, what?"

"Why were you pissed? He ain't your man, Leigh. He can fuck whoever he wants."

"I wasn't mad about that. My name is still on the lease, Myles, and my stuff is there. It's just disrespectful."

"You sure that's the only reason you mad?" he questioned.

"Oh my God! Are you for real? You've been blowing my back out, *literally,* since the day my engagement ended, and you think I'm worried about his ass?"

"Aye, I'm just askin'. You *were* about to *marry* the nigga."

"I was not about to marry him. I never even chose a wedding date. Every chance you get, you throw that shit in my face. I don't wanna talk about that anymore."

Neither of them spoke for a minute. Everleigh was annoyed that Myles brought up that she was engaged to Easton. It obviously bothered him more than he let on.

"I called to hear your voice and see your face. I wasn't trying to argue with you."

"My bad, baby. I took your anger about the situation the wrong way. What else did you do today?" he asked, changing the subject.

"Besides packing and catching up with my girls, nothing much. How about you?"

"I only had one car to detail, so it was a short day. After work, I went home, showered, then went over to the Boys and Girls Club for a couple hours and played basketball with the boys. I talked to a few of them about working part-time for me at the shop."

"Really? That's great, baby."

"It should be. After that, I had to take another shower before I took some food over to your pops and chilled with him for a few hours."

"I talked to my dad earlier, and he seemed to be in good spirits. Thank you for spending some time with him."

"Yeah, he was good when I left, and no need to thank me. I was hanging with Mr. Everette before you knew anything about it. Remember?"

"I do remember, and I love you even more for that. I also love that you volunteer. Once I get settled, I should go with you and see if there's something I can do."

"Me volunteering was all Ms. Dinah's idea."

"Really?"

"Yep, and I'm glad I listened. Those kids probably help me way more than I helped them. They're always lookin' for volunteers, baby. I'm sure there's plenty you can do. But hold up, before you left, you seemed undecided about movin' back."

"I just wanted to make you think I was," she teased.

"Oh, I always knew you were. I meant it when I said I'm not lettin' you go. I just wanted you to feel like it was your decision."

Everleigh shook her head at his comment. Myles had to be the bossiest man she'd ever dealt with, but she loved it.

"Whatever! Hey, when you were at my dad's house, did you happen to go in my bathroom?"

"No. Why? Wassup?"

"I could have sworn I packed my birth control pills, but they aren't in my purse."

"I threw 'em out."

"Huh? Wait. What?"

"I took your pills and threw 'em out," he repeated like it was nothing. "You said you would have my babies, and you can't do that if you takin' them damn pills, Leigh."

"Don't you think we should have had a conversation about that *before* you took the liberty of throwing my shit away?"

"I thought we did. I was disappointed when I saw you put them in your purse. Look, you almost thirty-five, and I'll be thirty-eight soon. We need to get started."

Everleigh considered what he said, and although he did make a lot of sense, she didn't think he should have thrown her pills away without speaking to her first.

"Anything that is said while you're knee-deep inside me is questionable. I'm not saying that it should be completely disregarded, but a real conversation should be had after the fact. Agreed?"

"If you say so, baby," he replied, dismissing her. "Aye, I told Jory I'd meet up with him for a couple rounds of pool. I ain't seen my boy since I opened the shop."

"Jory?"

"Yeah, you remember him?"

"Yeah, umm, I do. You and him still cool?"

"Why wouldn't we be?" he questioned. Everleigh could give him a few reasons to end that so-called friendship.

"Oh, umm...does he...is he still..."

"Yeah, he is, but I know how to handle myself, baby. We just goin' to play pool. If it's not too late, I'll call you when I get in."

"I don't care how late it is, call me. Okay?"

"Okay. I love you."

"Love you more."

Everleigh ended the call and went back into the living room, only to find that Robbie and Layne had fallen asleep on either end of the couch. She turned the TV off and tapped Robbie, waking her up. Without a word, she got up and went to her bedroom. After covering Layne with the throw blanket that was on the back of the couch, she went back to the guest bedroom and fell into a fitful sleep. Hearing Jory's name stirred something inside her, bringing certain memories to the forefront of her mind, even while she slept.

Everleigh pulled into her spot in the parking garage of the high rise building she shared with Myles. She hated Wednesdays because she had a night class and didn't get home until ten.

"Yo, Ev!" she heard after closing her car door.

Everleigh turned around to see Jory, a friend of Myles'. She wondered what he was doing there since he didn't live in the building. Jory was not someone that she was fond of, even though she had no legitimate reason not to like him. Her gut told her that he was bad news, and that was all she needed to form her opinion about him. She was sure to grip the can of mace that was attached to her keys, just in case he was on some bullshit.

"Jory? What are you doing here?"

He looked around as he approached her. No one else seemed to be in the garage, but she knew there were cameras, which only made her feel slightly safer. Jory didn't speak until he was a few feet in front of her.

"I heard you puttin' pressure on my boy," he said in a very low voice.

"How is that your business?"

"We came in this shit together, always said we leavin' together, and I ain't ready to leave."

"That sounds like your problem, not ours."

He chuckled and brushed his thumb under his nose.

"You always have had a real slick mouth. If you was my bitch, I'd slap the—"

"First of all, I ain't nobody's bitch. Now, why are you here?"

Another chuckle followed a deep breath. Jory had it bad for Everleigh... real bad. So bad, that he pleasured himself regularly to visions of her. He was sure that had Myles not approached her first, she'd be head over heels in love with him, instead of his boy. The only thing he wanted more than Everleigh was money. Right now, her influence on Myles had the potential to mess up his money, and he didn't like that, which made her an enemy.

"I need him out here, and you fuckin' that up with all that shit you talkin' in his ear. He so sprung over that pussy, he gon' do whatever you say. You got three months."

"Three months to what?"

"Get his head back in the game because if he bows out, not only will I make him regret it, you will too."

"When I tell him—"

"I wouldn't do that if I were you. If he has to choose between you and me, I have no doubt he'll choose you. But do you really wanna be the reason his life is cut short?"

Everleigh's expression changed from angry to shocked and confused. Jory was supposed to be Myles's best friend, and here he was threatening his life.

"This conversation stays here," he continued. "If I get the feelin' you said somethin', that cute little house on Crestwood, might go up in flames in the middle of the night."

She couldn't believe her ears. Not only didn't he threatened her and her man, but he also threatened her parents. If she had any doubts about the evil person that Jory was, he just made her a believer.

Everleigh popped up outta her sleep in a cold sweat. Grabbing her phone, she checked to see how long she had been asleep and if she had missed any calls or texts from Myles. It was just after midnight, and she debated whether or not she should call him or send him a text. It was about ten when they ended their call, so he hadn't been out for very long. Opting to send a text, she went to his contact.

Me: Hey, you still out?

While she waited for him to reply, she went to the kitchen to get a glass of water, then used the bathroom before she returned to bed. When she checked her phone, he still hadn't replied. She scrolled her Instagram page while she waited for him to respond and ended up falling back into a restless sleep.

"Everleigh!"

Without turning in the direction of the voice, she knew who it was. Hearing him made her cringe. She never liked Jory, but since he approached her in the parking garage of the condo, she hated him with a passion. Instead of going his way, she went in the opposite direction. He followed and cornered her in a secluded area.

"Why are you here?"

She had just walked out of one of her classes at SCCC, and the fact that Jory was there waiting didn't sit well with her.

"I figured it was time for us to revisit our conversation. Time is tickin', and our boy ain't changed his tune. He still tryin' to get out."

"I can't change his mind, not now. He wants out just as much as I want him out."

"And I told you to change his mind. You know, it would be a shame if somethin' happened to your parents on their daily walk."

Instead of replying, she shoved past him and race-walked down the hall.

"You got one month," she heard him yell to her back.

Again, she popped up out of her sleep, and her heart was racing. Her phone had fallen onto her lap, and she picked it up to see that Myles had returned her text.

My Nigga: I'm home. We can talk tomorrow. Love you

The clock read three-thirty-five, and she was surprised that she had been asleep that long. Since she knew Myles had to get up for work, she decided not to bother him. Knowing he was home safe was enough to allow her to get a few more hours of sleep. This time, it was a much more restful slumber.

CHAPTER 16

Myles met Jory at Temple Billiard, one of the pool halls in town. He was still heavy in the streets, and since Myles no longer partook in those activities and spent the majority of his time at his shop, they hadn't connected in quite a while. One thing he realized as he transitioned into his new lifestyle, was that he didn't have friends. The people he once thought were his friends didn't really fuck with him because they didn't understand why he wanted a change. The further away he was from the streets, the less he saw them, until he stopped seeing them altogether. Some might think he would be lonely but he enjoyed the time alone.

"Aww, shit. Look who graced me with his presence," Jory teased when he noticed Myles. "I thought you might be a no show."

"Shut the hell up, nigga," he replied as they gave each other some dap and a one-armed hug. "What's been up? You been straight?"

"Same shit every day, bruh. Ain't nothin' changed for nobody but you," Jory replied.

Something about his tone didn't sit right with Myles, but he let it slide.

"I guess not. You still doin' the same shit, so ain't shit gon' change."

"Everybody ain't tryin' to be a model citizen," Jory said with a shrug of his shoulders. "Shop must be keepin' you busy as hell."

"I can't complain. Business is good. Great, actually, but my ass be tired at the end of the day."

"Lil different from the old line of work, huh. Havin' regrets?"

"Naw, not at all. Probably the best decision I ever made. Wish I hadn't waited so long."

"Real talk?" Jory asked, surprised for some reason.

"Hell, yeah. The only thing I regret is not walkin' away when I was plannin' to the first time. I'd be married with a house full of kids by now."

"Damn, bruh. You still stuck on her," Jory said as he racked up the balls. "Her pussy must have been—"

Myles hopped in his face so quick, he stopped talking midsentence.

"The fuck you say?"

Jory took a couple steps back and put his hands up in surrender.

"My bad, bruh. I ain't know you was still attached. She left your ass. Remember?"

Myles backed off and took a few deep breaths. "Yeah, she did, but she's back, and I ain't lettin' her ass go this time."

"Hold up. Everleigh's back?"

"Her mom passed away almost two months ago, and she's been home since then."

"Damn! I'm, uhh, I'm sorry to hear that. So what, y'all just picked up where y'all left off?"

"Pretty much. I mean, she was engaged to some nigga she met in L.A., but she gave his ass his ring back before I even had to tell her."

Jory shook his head before saying, "You a way better nigga than me, bruh. Ain't no way no bit—I mean woman gon' leave me without warning, and we be cool again."

"It was a long time ago, and I'm over it, bruh. She had her reasons, and it is what it is."

"Wait! She umm, she told you why she left?" Myles nodded. "What'd she tell you?"

Myles thought he noticed something in Jory's demeanor change like he suddenly became nervous, but he had no reason to be, so Myles brushed it off.

"Nothin' new. We haven't even talked about it, specifically. I know why she left, and I don't feel the need to revisit it. I'm about to marry her ass and plant as many seeds as I can between now and when she turns forty."

Jory seemed to have tuned Myles out and was focused on the pool game. For the next few hours, they played pool, and ordered some food, and conversed about random things. When Myles made it home, he pulled out his phone to call Everleigh but saw that she had sent him a text. Instead of calling her, he replied to the text and went to bed.

The next morning, he was awakened by his phone. When he saw Everleigh was Facetiming him, he answered the call.

"Baby, what time is it?" he answered.

"It's early, but you didn't call me when you got in last night."

"'I sent you a text 'cause I ain't wanna wake you up like you doin' me now. You good?"

"I'm fine. Call me when you get up."

"Aight, I love you."

"Love you more."

Myles's first client of the day wouldn't be dropping his car off until nine, so he went back to sleep for a few more hours.

MYLES PULLED UP AT HIS SHOP AND ENDED HIS CALL WITH Everleigh. About five minutes later, his client walked in. After discussing the specifics and leaving his keys, he left with the ride that was waiting for him. Once Myles got started on the car, time flew by. At about noon, he was about three-quarters of the way done with the car. When he heard the bell above the shop door sound, he went to see who it was.

"Wassup?" Jory said when Myles walked in.

"Just workin' on finishin' up a car. You good? I just saw your ass last night."

"Oh, I'm straight. Figured I'd stop by and check you out."

Jory looked around the front area, which wasn't a whole lot, then made eye contact with Myles.

"As you can see, it ain't much. You can come see the garage area if you want, but it ain't much either."

Myles went back through the door he entered, with Jory behind him. Jory looked around and nodded his head.

"It's a nice lil spot," he commented.

"'Preciate that, bruh. Aye, but I gotta get this car done before the owner gets back to pick it up."

"My bad. I ain't wanna hold you up, but I did wanna ask a favor."

"Wassup?"

He looked around again before he spoke. "Can I put a stash here?"

"A stash of what, nigga?" Myles asked, although he knew precisely what Jory was talking about.

Jory cocked his head to the side because he knew Myles knew what he was asking.

Shaking his head, Myles replied, "You really puttin' me in this position?"

"I wouldn't ask if I ain't need to, bruh. You know we can't trust too many out here, not even the ones on our team."

Myles released a deep breath. He wanted to ask more details but didn't want to get too involved. Jory was his boy, and they'd always looked out for each other.

"For how long?"

"About a week."

"Let me think about it. I'll hit you up tonight."

"Cool. It won't be until next week. Take a few days and let me know. I'm out so you can get back to work."

They dapped each other up, and Jory left, while Myles got back to work, with Jory's request heavy on his mind. The more removed Myles became from the streets, the less he and Jory communicated. Once MAAD opened, communication stopped altogether. When

Myles thought back to the previous night, Jory's odd demeanor came to mind. He wondered if the reason Jory reached out to him in the first place was to ask him this favor. There was a time when he wouldn't hesitate to help his boy out, but something felt off about this. His gut was telling him to steer clear.

CHAPTER 17

Everleigh reached out to Easton and had arranged for him to meet her at her studio. He tried to get out of it, but after going back and forth briefly, he agreed to come at three o'clock.

The photoshoot she had scheduled ran very smoothly. It had been a couple of months since she'd worked, and she hadn't realized how much she missed it. She was anxious to get settled in Seattle and back to a regular work schedule. After the client and his people left, she got right to editing the pictures. Before she knew it, an hour had passed. She'd gotten through most of the edits and was confident she'd have them back to the client before she went back to Seattle.

There was still another hour or so before Easton would arrive, so she made a note of all the equipment she'd have to move, then made a few phone calls, one of them being to the owner of the studio space. She was very gracious regarding Everleigh's situation and offered her a few options, giving her a couple of weeks to decide. Before she knew it, she heard the buzzer and looked at the security monitor to see Easton at the door. When she heard him enter, she called out, letting him know she was in her office.

"Come on in and have a seat," she told him when he stopped just shy of entering.

As soon as he sat in the chair in front of Everleigh's desk, he began with an apology for the previous night.

"Ev, before we even get started, I want to apologize for yesterday. I know it must have hurt you to see me with someone else. I—"

"Let me just stop you right there. I appreciate your apology, but I don't want you to get it confused. When I gave that ring back, it meant that we were no longer together. You are free to fuck whoever you want. What you should be apologizing for is having her all up in my shit. That's still my home, Easton, and that was disrespectful as hell."

"I thought we were just taking a break."

"You thought wrong. And if that's what you thought, that makes what you did even more fucked up. But I didn't ask you here to talk about that. I'm moving back to Seattle, and we need to discuss what to do with the condo."

"You're moving back to Seattle?" he asked, with an expression of hurt and surprise on his face.

"That's what I said. We can sell it and split the money down the middle, or you can buy me out. All I want are my clothes and personal items, and you can keep everything else."

"How is this so easy for you? We were together for three years and engaged to be married. You're saying this like I meant nothing to you."

Everleigh almost felt bad, then she thought about how he went ghost when her mother died.

"Were we engaged when you put me on your private jet, by myself, to come and see about my mother? Were we engaged when you didn't call me to make sure she was okay? Were we engaged when you found out she died and were too busy to hop on that same private jet to make sure I was okay?"

"Ev, that was one incident. I—"

"One incident? My mother is *dead,* you asshole. She didn't fall and break her hip, *she's dead!* But since you don't think that 'incident' is enough to make ending this relationship easy, I got a few more. Let's talk about the time I had pneumonia, and you couldn't push back your business trip to make sure I was okay. How about the time someone rear-ended me, totaling my car, and instead of coming to the ER to make sure I was okay, you sent your mother? Then, there was the time—"

"Okay, okay! Damn! I didn't know you were keeping tabs on everything I did wrong. People make mistakes, Ev. If my actions were a problem, you should have told me then instead of holding a grudge. You—"

"First of all, I'm too damn old to be holding a grudge. Secondly, why should I have to tell my man when it's appropriate to be there for me? That's something you should just know. It should be second nature."

They sat in silence, staring each down. Everleigh felt like she'd said all she needed to say. All she wanted from him now was to know what he wanted to do with the condo. When Easton didn't seem to have a word to say, she continued.

"Look, Easton, we were friends before anything else. I don't want to argue with you about the past. We've both moved on and—"

"You went back to your ex, didn't you? I knew it! How long did it take for you to hop on his dick, Ev?"

"You know what, Easton, get the fuck out. I'll have my lawyer contact yours, and we can figure this out that way. I'm done!"

He shot up from the chair and leaned over the desk, with anger in his eyes.

"Admit it! You've been fucking him this whole time. That's why you never set a wedding date. All those trips you took home were to see him, and you were just stringing me along."

Everleigh matched Easton's energy and stood from her seat as well. He was at least a foot taller than her, but since he was leaning toward her, they were almost face-to-face.

"I wasn't," she said slowly. "But with that weak ass dick of yours, I wish I was."

Before he could stop himself, the palm of his right hand went across the left side of Everleigh's face. It landed so hard that it knocked her back into the chair, causing it to roll back, just enough to make her head hit the wall behind her. One hand went to her face, the other went to the back of her head, as she tried to register what had just occurred. Her eyes began to fill with tears from the pain and shock of the situation.

"Oh shit, Ev!"

He rushed to her aid, but when he got near her, she wildly kicked both feet in his direction, and he backed up.

"Ev, I swear I didn't mean to hit you. I'm so sorry!"

"Leave, Easton! Now!" she demanded, as she felt her face and head begin to swell.

"I just want to make sure you're okay."

"If you don't get out! Just get out, now!"

After a few tense moments, he finally left. Everleigh kept her eyes on the security system, and once she was sure he was gone, she breathed a sigh of relief. She made her way to the bathroom, and just as she thought, her jaw was already swollen and bruised.

"I can't believe this nigga hit me," she said to the mirror.

Although she couldn't see the back of her head, she felt the knot that had formed. The longer she looked at her face, the angrier she got. Digging her phone from her back pocket, she took pictures of her face from every angle. It was hard to get the back of her head because her hair was covering up the swollen area.

Just as she was about to request an Uber to take her to the police station, Myles's face popped up on her screen with a FaceTime call.

"Great!"

She decided to ignore the call, and when it stopped ringing, she sent him a text. If Myles found out that Easton hit her, there was no telling what he would do.

Me: Can I call you later

My Nigga: When

Me: When I leave the studio

My Nigga: Ain't the shoot over

Me: Yeah but I'm in the middle of something

Instead of texting her back, he FaceTimed her again.

"Shit!"

This time she answered but didn't look directly into the phone.

"Hey, baby!" she answered, trying to sound cheerful.

"Leigh, I'm not tryin' to talk to the damn ceiling."

She picked up the phone but kept it positioned so that he could only see the right side of her face.

"Is that better?" she said with a forced smile.

"No, it's not. Wassup? You good?"

"I'm fine. I was just, umm, was organizing the studio."

"Aye, baby, hold the phone right so I can see your pretty face. You can get back to work in a few. I got some good news."

Slowly, she moved the phone to a position that allowed Myles to see her whole face. She automatically closed her eyes and waited for the shit to hit the fan.

"What the fuck happened to your face, Leigh?"

"I, umm, met with Easton and—"

"Did he—fuck! Did you call twelve?"

"No, I was—"

"Don't!"

Without another word, he ended the call. *This will not end well...at all.*

HOURS LATER, EVERLEIGH WAS READY TO LEAVE HER STUDIO. Luckily, Layne had a late night at the office and could pick her up. It was close to eight in the evening, but there was still some light left in the day. She still couldn't believe what had transpired that afternoon and early evening and was nervous about what would likely happen in a matter of hours. Based on the conversation she had with her father after Myles ended their call, she had reason to be.

When she tried to call Myles back, he kept ignoring her calls. After about fifteen minutes, she called her father to see if she could talk him through connecting a three-way call with Myles. However, when her father picked up, Myles could be heard in the background.

"I'm gon' kill that nigga," Myles shouted.

"Daddy, please let me talk to him. I have to calm him down."

"He's as calm as he's gon' get, for right now, baby girl. If I was a few years

younger, I'd be booking a flight to come and beat Easton's ass, myself. Please tell me this was the first time he put his hands on you."

"It was, Daddy, but can I talk to Myles?"

"He doesn't want to talk to you right now, Ev. He's leaving shortly for the airport."

"Oh my God! I know he wants to get his hands on Easton, but his family is wealthy, and they know a lot of people. I don't want Myles to come here and get arrested, or worse. Please, Daddy, give him the phone."

"I'll talk to him, baby girl, but he's gon' do what he's gon' do."

"He doesn't even know where my condo or my studio is. Where is he going when lands?"

"I'll talk to you later, Ev. I love you."

After the other man in her life hung up in her face, she sat in disbelief for a good thirty minutes before she went to the kitchenette and found some ice packets for her head and face. It sounded to her like her father was encouraging Myles right into an assault and battery charge, maybe more, and that surprised her. She knew that when Myles found out what Easton had done, he would lose it. It wasn't that she didn't think that Easton needed a good ass whooping, she just didn't want Myles to get in any legal trouble.

Just when she thought the craziness was over for the day, she heard the buzzer, indicating someone was requesting entrance to the studio. Looking at the monitor, she cringed when she saw that it was Mrs. Briggs.

"What else can happen today?" she said aloud.

Everleigh generally didn't have an issue with Easton's mother, and they'd always gotten along well. However, Shelby could be a bit much, and considering everything that had already happened since she'd touched down in L.A., she was banking on this visit not going well. She buzzed her in and met her in the front area.

"Hi, sweet—what happened to your face? Did you fall?"

"No, actually. Your son didn't like something I said, so he decided to slap me across my face."

"Noooo! Easton did this? What in the world?"

"Yes, Easton did this, and I haven't decided if I'm gonna press charges or not."

"Has that boy completely lost his mind? He hasn't—tell me this hasn't been abusing you all this time. Is that why—"

"No, Mrs. Briggs, Easton has never put his hands on me in this way. I wouldn't stand for it, and you'd probably be childless."

"Oh, thank God! I know Easton isn't perfect, but I didn't raise an abuser. This is still inexcusable. Everleigh, I don't know what to say, an apology isn't nearly enough. I do understand if you want to press charges, but I'm begging you to reconsider."

Everleigh's face went into a deep frown as she folded her arms across her chest and put all of her weight on her right leg.

"Why would I reconsider? Don't you think he needs to be punished?"

"I do, but not at the expense of my company. I can't allow his irresponsible actions to ruin what I've worked so hard to build up and maintain after his father died. I don't condone what he did at all, but please consider the lives that will be affected if this gets out."

For now, she didn't have to worry about Everleigh calling the police because Myles told her not to. However, she had pictures and video camera footage of him entering and leaving her studio. She wouldn't hesitate to use it at a later time. She also knew that whatever Myles had planned would probably be punishment enough.

When Everleigh didn't say anything, Shelby continued with her pleas. "Sweetheart, I know this is asking a lot, and it probably makes me seem insensitive. Is there—"

"I hold off on doing anything, for now. However, if he gives me any trouble with selling the condo, or buying me out, I may reconsider."

"Whatever you need him to do, he'll do it. If you want to use the company jet to move all your belongings back to Seattle, it's all yours."

"How did you know that I was moving back?"

"Because if I saw the way you and your ex looked at each other. You'd be a fool not to."

Mrs. Briggs approached her with open arms and gave her a tight hug.

"I like you for Easton, but he doesn't know what to do with a woman like you. I hoped and prayed he would figure it out before you realized that you two weren't a good fit. He doesn't know how to love you, and it's probably my fault. Everything is always the mother's fault," she said with an uncomfortable laugh. "If you ever need anything, feel free to reach out. I'll make sure everything is set up with the jet."

Since a few minutes after the door closed behind Mrs. Briggs,

Everleigh had been sitting at her desk, trying to decompress from the day's events. When Layne arrived, she activated the alarm, then locked up her studio. As soon as her butt hit the passenger seat, she released a deep sigh.

"Oh boy. Sounds like you had a rough day."

Without responding, she turned on the interior light of the car to give Layne a better look at her face.

"What in the entire fuck happened to your face?"

"You wouldn't believe me if I told you."

"I'm listening."

CHAPTER 18

T he minute Myles ended the call with Everleigh, after finding out that Easton had put his hands on her, he checked the flights. Unfortunately, the next flight going to L.A. wasn't for a few hours. That gave him some time to reschedule the appointments he had for the next two days. When that was done, he grabbed a duffle bag and threw some clothes and essentials inside, then went and bought a burner phone, before going to see Mr. Everette.

Myles didn't have much to tell Mr. Everette about what happened between his daughter and Easton. All he knew was that Easton hit Everleigh in her face. Mr. Everette was upset, and willingly gave Myles the name of the company Easton's family owned, the address of the condo he shared with Everleigh, and his cell phone number.

When Everleigh called her father, Myles was ranting in the background, and she heard him. Myles refused to speak to her because he knew she would try to talk him out of his plans, although with the way he was feeling, he didn't think that was possible. Myles powered down his personal cell phone and gave it to Mr. Everette, then parked his truck in the garage. Using Mr. Everette's phone, he requested an Uber. While they waited, Mr. Everette had some time to calm down and think logically, then he spoke his peace about what he assumed was about to happen.

"Look, son, I know you're upset. I am, too. But before you leave, I need you to do me a favor."

"I'm listenin'."

"Think about my Dinah and what she would say to you right now. As men, our first instinct is to protect the ones we love. You're not the man you used to be, son. You have to figure out other ways to solve your problems now. You and Ev are planning a future together. You're a business owner, and you got those boys at the club looking up to you. Things are different because you're different. Don't go out there and do something that will jeopardize all that you've worked to become."

Myles only nodded because he didn't want to acknowledge that Mr. Everett was right. He only knew one way to solve a problem like this.

"You know, Easton is not of the streets. If something happens to him, people will want to know what happened. His family has enough money to turn over every rock and look into every lead until they find answers. I'm not telling you what to do. I just want you to think about it."

Myles heard every word, but at the moment, he wasn't sure if he'd take heed. Thankfully, the Uber pulled up, and he didn't have to give a lengthy response.

"I hear you, Mr. Everette. I'll see you when I get back."

WHEN MYLES LANDED, IT WAS A LITTLE AFTER ELEVEN AT NIGHT. He booked a room at a hotel near LAX, using a different alias than he used to book his flight. From his previous lifestyle, Myles had a few identities that he used when he traveled for criminal activities. He didn't use them often, but for what he had planned on this trip, he thought it was necessary.

After reaching out to his boy that lived in Santa Monica, which was only about twenty minutes away, he waited. About an hour later, a text came through, alerting him that Droop had arrived. When he got outside, he saw the headlights of a car flash once, and he headed in that direction. Once he slid inside, he turned to face him.

"The fuck is up with you, nigga? I thought you was done with this street shit," Droop greeted as they gave each other some dap.

Myles had known Droop all his life. They grew up on the same block, went to the same high school, and ran the same streets. His government name was Terry, but he was nicknamed Droop because of how low his eyes always were. About five years ago, Droop fell in love with the woman who is now his wife. She didn't agree with his lifestyle, even though most of Droop's illegal activities were on the technology side. When she gave him an ultimatum, unlike Myles, he wasted no time making his exit. Droop, and his wife moved to L.A. and haven't looked back since.

"I am, bruh, but check this out. You remember, Leigh?"

"Leigh? Everleigh, your ex-girl?" he confirmed as he pulled out of the hotel parking lot.

"Yeah, well, as of a couple months ago, she's not my ex."

"Oh, word? That's cool. I know you had it bad for her. Glad y'all could work it out after all that time."

"Yeah, me too. She was engaged to this corporate nigga while she was livin' out here. She flew in a couple days ago to get things squared away with the condo they had and her photography studio. She met up with him and he put his hands on her."

"That explains why you had to come outta retirement. Whatchu need?"

"I got his cell number. I need to find out where this nigga be and when...see if he got some kinda routine."

"Oh, that's it? That's easy."

Droop reached in the backseat and grabbed his laptop. Myles watched as he opened it and did a bunch of shit that he didn't understand.

"You can do that shit right here?" Myles asked.

"Technology is a beautiful thing, bruh. Real talk, I could probably do this shit from my phone, but I wanna point out some shit to you on a bigger screen. What's his number?"

Myles reached in his pocket for the piece of paper the number was on and read it off to him.

"Gimme two minutes."

Droop did his thing, and as he said, about two minutes later, he turned the screen toward Myles.

"Bruh livin' nice. What you say he do?"

"Briggs Real Estate...his family owns it," Myles replied.

"Oh, word. That's a Fortune 500 company. Okay, look here. This nigga boring as hell. Basically, does the exact same thing every day."

Droop pointed out that Easton leaves his house at about five-thirty each morning. Based on what he could decipher, he runs through the streets of downtown. He told Myles that his best bet would be to find one of the smaller streets on his route and catch him there.

"Or, I can deactivate the security, including the cameras, in his building for a brief time, and you can be waiting for him in the condo when he gets back."

"Nigga! Why the fuck you ain't just say that in the first place?"

Droop shrugged his shoulders before saying, "I ain't know how adventurous you wanted to get. Okay, so here's what we should do..."

About twenty minutes later, Myles was back in his hotel room. It was now close to one a.m., so he set the alarm clock on the bedside table for four. He laid down to get a few hours of sleep, confidant that the plan that he and Droop put together would work.

WHAT FELT LIKE MINUTES LATER, THE ALARM SOUNDED. He popped up, a bit disoriented, and it took him a second to remember where he was. He'd only been asleep for about three hours, but strangely, he felt rested. After sending Droop a text message, reminding him to send the Uber his way, he used the bathroom and rinsed his mouth out with some mouthwash. He left the hotel room and headed for the Uber that was waiting.

It was still dark outside, but as Myles approached the car, it looked as if someone was in the backseat. He wasn't too familiar with the app, but he was sure you could request to ride alone. Droop probably didn't think about that at this early hour. Deciding it wasn't that big of a deal, he opened the driver's side back door and saw the absolute last person he was expecting to see.

CHAPTER 19

Everleigh woke up at the crack of dawn, after a night of tossing and turning. Her gut had been telling her that something was about to go down, but she had no idea what it was or where it would happen. What she did know was who would be involved.

After speaking with her father the day before, she knew that Myles was in L.A. by now. She called him and left messages until the voicemail was full. At that point, all that she could do was wait and hope that he would reach out to her. But after a night of restless sleep, her anxiety was at an all-time high because she knew Myles was about to do something drastic.

On a whim, she grabbed her phone from the bedside table and requested an Uber. Hopping out of bed, she dressed in a pair of leggings and hoodie, then went to wash the sleep out of her eyes and brush her teeth. When she glanced in the mirror, she was startled by what she saw. The bruising had moved to the area around her eye, and it looked much worse than it felt. It didn't hurt nearly as much as she thought it would. After finishing up in the bathroom, she wrote a note for Layne and Robbie and taped it to the guestroom door, then grabbed her purse and phone before leaving.

Minutes later, the Uber pulled up in front of Robbie's house. When she was settled in the backseat, the driver turned his slightly to speak to her.

"You didn't indicate that you wanted to ride alone, and I have a pick-up request that's going to the same area as you. Do you mind?"

She shook her head as she replied, "No, it's fine."

Everleigh would use the long ride to calm her nerves and figure out what she would do if she actually walked in on a crime scene. She tuned out the sounds of the music the driver was playing and was in a world of her own. She hadn't even noticed when the driver pulled into the parking lot of a hotel until the back door on the driver's side opened. Her head turned in that direction, and her hand went to her chest when her eyes met the new passenger.

"Leigh, what the fuck?"

"Myles, I've been calling you."

Myles could not believe his luck. He would have bet everything he owned, and then some that something like this could never happen. His first thought was that God had to be trying to tell him something, and at the moment, all he could do was listen. There is no way he could follow through with his plan now that Everleigh was in his presence.

"Get out!" he commanded her.

"What?"

"Get out and come with me," he repeated before closing the door and walking back towards the hotel.

She hurriedly got out and jogged to catch up with him. They didn't speak until they were in Myles's hotel room. Everleigh sat on the bed and watched Myles as he paced back and forth for a brief moment. Stopping in front of her, he softly gripped her chin and brushed his thumb across her bruised cheek.

"It doesn't feel as bad as it looks," she told him.

"I don't care how the fuck it feels. That nigga put his hands on you, and he has to pay. Was this the first time—"

"Yes, it was, and he will pay but not if it means you doing something to jeopardize your freedom."

"Baby—"

"No, Myles, I'll press charges or blast him on social media, but I won't let you do something crazy."

"It's not—"

His phone began to vibrate, interrupting him.

"Shit," he said before answering. "You not gon' believe this shit."

Because it was so quiet in the room, Everleigh could hear the person Myles was speaking to.

"The fuck you at, bruh?"

"I'm still at the hotel. When the damn Uber pulled up, guess who was inside."

"Man, I don't know."

"My girl, nigga! I gotta put shit on pause for now. I'll hit you up later."

"Hold up! You said—"

"Later, bruh! I'll call you."

Myles ended the call before anything else could be said, then gave his attention back to Everleigh.

"How did you know I was here?" he asked, sitting next to her on the bed.

"Who was that?"

"Don't worry about that, right now. Answer my question."

"How would I know you were here? This ain't nothing but God trying to stop you from doing something stupid."

"What I was about to do was far from stupid. The nigga—"

"I know, baby, and I'm pissed as hell. I would have already pressed charges if it weren't for you. If Easton is gonna pay, we have to think of another way."

"That ain't how I handle shit, baby."

"It may not be how you used to handle shit, but you're not the same person you used to be. I took pictures, and I have security footage of him entering and leaving my studio. I can go to the police station right now and press charges."

Myles sat in deep thought, trying to convince himself that killing Easton, or at least injuring him severely, was not the right thing to do. It was hard to do because every time he looked at Everleigh's face, he was convinced that Easton should die. His hand went to her bruised cheek again, and he leaned forward to softly planted a kiss there before his mouth moved to her lips. His free hand went to caress her other cheek, and he kissed her hard and with passion, but with no tongue. Just their lips joined together, communicating the love they had for each other. When they separated, they were both breathless.

"Come shower with me," he told her before standing and heading the bathroom.

"You don't want to go to the police station?"

For now, his solution was feeling her tight, wet walls, wrapped around his dick. The peace he was seeking about the situation was between her thighs, and being inside her would calm his racing mind. Ignoring her question, he started the shower and undressed. When he turned to face Everleigh, and she hadn't started to take her clothes off, he grabbed the hem of the hoodie she was wearing and pulled it up. She lifted her arms, and it went over her head, then landed on the floor.

"Take this shit off," Myles commanded as the tugged at the waist-band of her leggings.

Without further delay, she stripped out of her clothing and stepped into the shower, where he was already waiting. As the water rained down around him and the bathroom filled with a thin layer of steam, she looked up into his eyes. In them, she saw the love he had for her, and it sent chills through her body.

He pulled her into his hard chest and said, "For you, I would kill him without a second thought."

Everleigh nodded as tears filled her eyes. Knowing that Myles loved her so much that he'd go to that extent was overwhelming. He'd always loved her that way, and she hated that she allowed herself to be bullied into leaving him. Until his confession, the night their bodies reunited, she had no idea that he felt like she had given up on him, and that he wasn't worthy of her love. She wanted to tell him the real reason she left, to let him know that it wasn't him, that she didn't give up on him, and that he was more than worthy, but didn't want to open up a can of worms.

Their lips met again, but this time, when their tongues fought to connect. Myles backed her up against the shower wall, and as his dick rubbed up against her stomach, he couldn't resist the need to be inside her. He palmed her ass and lifted her up, then slammed her onto his waiting dick.

"Ahhh," she cried out.

"For you, I'm gon' let him live."

Relief washed over Everleigh's body as Myles began to bury himself deep inside her womb, each stroke going deeper than the one before. When her head fell to his chest, she tightened the grip she had around his neck and tried to press her body as close to his as humanly possible. As they made the most intense, heated, and passionate love they'd made since they reunited, Everleigh couldn't contain her emotions. The deeper he dove, the more tears she shed.

As her pussy clenched tightly around his throbbing erection, Myles was having a hard time controlling the speed at which his nut was building. He wasn't ready to release his legacy inside of her. If he could, he would fuck her until the water ran cold, and their skin was wrinkled like a prune. However, his dick had other plans. No matter where his brain tried to steer his thoughts, they ended up right back on how sensational Everleigh pussy felt as it milked him of seeds.

"Baby, oh my Goooddd, I'm cummin'," she screamed.

That was music to his ears.

CHAPTER 20

After their lovemaking session in the shower, Myles and Everleigh slept until after noon. She woke up to several missed calls and text messages from Layne and Robbie. After replying to them in their group text, letting them know that she was with Myles and alive, and well, she sat her phone on the bedside table and rolled over to find Myles awake. His hand went to her bruised cheek, and he rubbed it softly.

"Tell me what happened?"

"Okay, let me go rinse my mouth out first."

She moved to get up, but Myles held her place.

"You know I don't care about your breath, baby. Tell me what happened."

Morning breath and all, she told him what led up to Easton slapping her across the face. Anger filled his eyes, but he remained calm.

"When messing with a man's ego, especially a weak man, they lose control. That might have been the first time he showed you that side of him, but I can guarantee that nigga would have shown his true colors once y'all got married."

"You think so. I just can't see—"

"I know so." He paused. "I got a plan, though."

"And what's that?"

"Reach out to him and tell him to meet you at your studio. When we meet him—"

"We?"

"Hell, yeah, *we*! You think I'm lettin' you be alone with this nigga?"

"I guess not."

"Just get him to your studio, and I'll handle it from there."

"So, what's the plan?"

"You'll find out soon enough, but don't worry, there's no violence involved. I told you, I ain't gon' kill his ass."

۞

A FEW HOURS LATER, THE MEETING WITH EASTON WAS CONFIRMED. They would be meeting at the end of his workday, which was about seven p.m. That gave Everleigh plenty of time to go back to Robbie's house and change clothes, and of course, let them grill her about her whereabouts.

After a few rounds of lovemaking before showering...and in the shower, the two finally left the hotel. Myles planned to meet up with his boy, Droop, who didn't live far from Robbie, so he and Everleigh shared an Uber. When it pulled in front of Robbie's house, Myles got out, then reached inside for Everleigh's hand to help her out. Leaning back inside the car, he told the Uber drive to wait while he walked her to the door.

"You mind if I meet your friends?" he asked.

"Of course not. I'm sure they're dying to meet you."

"You told them about me?"

"I left *some* things out, but yeah, they know all about you."

As soon as she let herself in, Layne and Robbie were in her face. They were so anxious to see Everleigh that, at first, they didn't notice Myles behind her. Layne was the first to see him, and she nudged Robbie, causing her to stop talking mid-sentence.

"Oh, umm, hi," Robbie greeted. "I'm Robbie; you must be Myles."

"I am. Nice to meet you." Myles extended his hand, as did Robbie before they shook.

His eyes went to Layne, who looked like she was starstruck, with her eyes and mouth wide open. When she didn't say anything, Everleigh introduced her.

"Baby, this is Layne. Apparently, her brain stopped working."

Layne still looked as if she was frozen in time. Robbie bumped her with her shoulder, and she finally came out of her daze.

"Hi, I'm Layne," she said, reintroducing herself.

"Nice to meet you," he replied with a smirk as he shook her hand. Turning to Everleigh, he wrapped her in his arms, and he said, "I'll see you in a few hours."

She nodded, then asked, "You got the address, right?"

"Yeah, I got it. I love you."

"I love you more."

Robbie and Layne were still standing within an arm's reach, but that didn't stop Myles from kissing his woman as if he'd just been sentenced to life in prison with no parole. Not until Layne and Robbie absently uttered "damn," simultaneously, did the two lovebirds disconnect. When Myles was on the other side of the door, Everleigh released a deep sigh and then leaned against it, waiting for one of her girls to speak.

"Why my damn panties wet?" Layne said, causing the three of them to burst out in laughter.

"Siiiisssss! You ain't tell us he was that damn fine!" Robbie exclaimed.

"Does he taste like chocolate? He looks like if I lick him, he'd taste like chocolate," Layne added.

"No, he looks like if you lick him, I'll beat the bricks off your ass."

Layne put her hand over her chest and pretended to be shocked.

"You would fight me over a nigga?" she said.

"No, I said I would beat the bricks off your ass over *that* nigga.

There would be no fight. I'd be tagging your ass so quick you wouldn't land a punch."

"Aww, shit! That's wassup! This some real love type shit right here. We used to talk about Easton's ass something terrible, and you ain't defend his ass one time," Layne said with a huge smile.

"Not even once!" Robbie confirmed. "But damn, Myles got any brothers? Cousins? Best friends? I'll take any male relatives."

"Hell, I'll take his daddy if he single," Layne added.

Everleigh was laughing so hard at the two of them. She had tears running down her eyes.

"He has a sister, and I've never met his father or any cousins." She shrugged her shoulders.

"Damn!" they said at the same time.

"I swear, y'all are crazy," Everleigh said, still laughing at their commentary.

"Okay, so we need to know what happened. Start from the time you left in the wee hours of the morning," Robbie said, pulling her over to the couch.

Unfortunately, Everleigh couldn't tell them the whole truth, which was that Myles had come to L.A. with the sole purpose of killing Easton. Instead, she told them that he hopped on a flight to make sure that she was okay and that he planned to give Easton the ass whooping he deserved. However, she was able to convince him to find a nonviolent way to get back at him because she didn't want him to risk his freedom. They seemed to be satisfied with that story, which was a relief.

"What's the plan when y'all meet up with him?" Robbie asked.

"He wouldn't tell me and told me I'd find out when we got there."

"You think he's gonna be able to restrain himself from beating the shit outta Easton? 'Cause every time I see those bruises on your face, I wanna blast his ass," Robbie shared.

"That remains to be seen. I hope so, though, because if they get to fighting, ain't shit I'm gon' be able to do."

"We should go with, you know, for—" Layne started.

"To be nosy," Everleigh interrupted, shaking her head. "Nope. If something goes down, we don't need witnesses."

The three of them broke out in laughter. Everleigh was genuinely going to miss them when she moved back to Seattle. They sat around talking for a little while longer, then Everleigh had to get ready for the meeting with Easton.

CHAPTER 21

When Myles arrived at Droop's house, his wife, Angie, answered the door. She was a tall redbone woman with short curly hair, and thick as hell. When they were in high school, not many girls found Droop very attractive, but somehow, he always pulled some of the baddest chicks. The two met when Angie moved to Seattle to live with her cousin. He pursued her with a vengeance and eventually wore her down. The rest is history.

"Myles, Terry told me you were in town. It's good to see you. Come on in."

Angie opened the door wider and moved to the side, allowing Myles the space he needed to go in.

"It's good to see you, too," he replied as they exchanged a friendly hug.

"Terry is up in his man cave. It's up the stairs and to your right. I gotta finish dinner before TJ wakes up from his nap. You're welcome to join us."

"Thank you. If I have time, I'll definitely stay."

He found the room with no problem. Droop had it decked out with a TV that was as big as the wall, computer monitors that looked like small TV's, a huge circular sectional couch that looked to include individual recliners. Myles hadn't given much thought to where or how he and Everleigh would be living once they got married, but seeing Droop's set up had him ready to put some thought into it. They'd definitely be buying a house sooner rather than later.

"Wassup, bruh!" Myles said as he entered the room.

"Wassup! I ain't think you were comin'. Sitcho ass down and tell me what the hell happened."

"You wouldn't believe this shit if you were driving the damn Uber."

"Word?"

Myles proceeded to tell him why he ended up not following through with their plan. Retelling the story didn't make it any more believable, and Droop's take on it confirmed what he'd thought the previous night, God was sending a message.

"You know I ain't a religious nigga, but I ain't no fool either. That was a sign, bruh. Accept that shit and move on."

"That's why I came with another plan. Well, that and Everleigh."

"Outstanding pussy will have the strongest nigga agreeing to damn near anything. Take it from me, I know." He shook his head, and they both chuckled, knowingly.

"What's your plan? 'Cause I know you ain't about to let his ass slide."

"So check it. You know I been volunteering with the Boys and Girls Club for a while."

Droop nodded. "Your ass was still heavy in the streets when you started that."

"I was, but a nigga needed to do some good in the hood." They both chuckled again. "Leigh took pictures of the bruises on her face when it happened. If he don't want them shits all over social media, he gotta agree to donate a million dollars to the club within the next week. Then follow that up with five hundred thousand every year for the next five years."

"Damn, bruh. You hittin' them pockets, but that's probably pennies to them," Droop reasoned.

"I know it is. They won't even miss it."

Myles ended up having an early dinner with Droop and Angie, and also met their two-year-old son, TJ. After dinner, Droop dropped him off at Everleigh's studio. Once inside, Everleigh gave him a quick tour. The space wasn't huge, and they ended up back in her office fairly quickly. He sat at the chair behind her desk, then pulled her onto his lap.

"This is nice, baby. Did you decide what to do with it?" he asked.

"I think I wanna keep it until my lease is up. I can work my schedule out and schedule multiple shoots during one visit. The flight is short enough that I can make a turnaround trip."

"That sounds like a good plan. The only issue you might have is when you're too pregnant to fly."

"What?"

"Ain't there some kind of limitations on flying when you pregnant. When Myla was pregnant with the twins—"

"Wait...she has twins?"

"Yep. I thought I told you. KJ and Mykha are two and a half now, and the baby, Kolana, is only a few months old."

"Wow! I couldn't imagine having three little ones so close in age."

"Lucky for you, you won't have to imagine it. You gon' be livin' it. I'm trying to knock you up asap. We probably won't have twins, but I hope you can handle back-to-back pregnancies."

Everleigh couldn't even respond as she processed how this man had made all these plans with her uterus, without having a conversation with her.

"Why you lookin' at me like that?"

Before she could tell him, the buzzer sounded. She looked at the monitor and saw Easton standing at the door. After pressing the button to allow him entry, she looked at Myles.

"Baby—"

"I ain't gon' do nothing to his punk ass," he said but was unsure of how true that was.

Easton walked into Everleigh's office and paused when he saw her sitting on Myles's lap. His body language expressed that he was pissed, but he didn't show it verbally.

"I didn't realize we'd have company," was all he said.

"Nigga, you lucky you still breathing right now. Sit the fuck down and shut up. You here to listen and agree. That's it."

Begrudgingly, Easton sat down. Everleigh was surprised at his attitude, considering the situation. But she decided to let her man handle everything.

"You will donate one million dollars to the Boys and Girls Club of Seattle by the end of next week, and five hundred thousand for the next five years. It will be donated in honor of Ms. Dinah, Everleigh's mother, and from your *personal* funds."

Everleigh looked at Myles with a huge smile on her face. She was pleased, and admittedly, a little turned on, by his new plan. Having the Briggs family donate such a large amount of money, money that they wouldn't miss at all, in honor of her mother was an amazing and thoughtful idea.

"What are you talking about?" Easton asked, obviously confused at the request.

"From what I understand, your mother doesn't want the police involved. She begged Leigh not to press charges."

Everleigh had shared with Myles the conversation she had with Mrs. Briggs. Surprisingly, he understood where she was coming from.

"Those are the terms. If you want to keep the police outta this, those are the terms," Myles reiterated when Easton didn't reply.

"You want me to donate three point five million dollars of *my* money? That's—"

"Is this your handprint on her face?"

"That was an accident. I lost it for one quick second and instantly regretted it."

"That one quick second is 'bout to cost you three point five mill over the next five years, or your reputation and your family's company. You lucky it didn't cost you your life, hell, it still can. You choose."

"Ev—"

"Don't address my woman. Do we have an agreement, or what?"

Easton was angry and using every ounce of restraint he had to contain it. He knew he was wrong for hitting Everleigh, but he wasn't an abuser and didn't want to be labeled as such. If his actions damaged his reputation and that of Briggs Real Estate, his mother would never forgive him.

"Fine," he agreed. "I assume one of you will get me the information I need to make it happen."

Without waiting for a reply from either of them, Easton wasted no time making his exit. Myles tapped Everleigh on the hip, indicating he wanted her to stand. Even though Myles seemed calm, she was hesitant to let him up. When she did, she grabbed him by his beard and pulled his face to hers.

"Behave," she told him before kissing his lips.

He gave her a smirk then left her office, catching Easton just as he made it to the door.

"I tried. I swear I did," Myles said, getting Easton's attention before he walked out.

Releasing an annoyed breath, Easton turned around to face Myles and find out what he was talking about.

"Tried what?"

"I tried to let you leave here without doing this."

With no other warning, Myles punched Easton right in the center of his face. Upon contact, a crack and a groan could be heard. Easton reached for his nose, that he was sure was broken, as he stumbled back and fell against the door.

"Myles, you promised," Everleigh gasped when Easton on the floor.

"I don't think I did, baby, but if so, I lied."

Myles didn't give a damn about the pain that Easton was experiencing. He pushed the door open and dragged him out of the studio.

"We'll be in touch," he said, before going back inside.

Everleigh looked at the door that she knew Easton was right outside of, probably still on the ground, groaning in pain. Releasing a deep sigh and shaking her head, she followed Myles back into her office. He was sitting at her desk like he didn't just break that man's nose.

"You couldn't resist, huh?"

"Fuck that nigga," he said, dismissively. "C'mere."

She went to him, but instead of sitting on his lap, like she was before and during the meeting with Easton, she stood facing him, with her butt against her desk.

"Lift up your dress."

Her hands went to her thighs, and slowly, she pulled the pink sundress up, until her thongs were revealed. Myles's hand reached for the thin, lace material and with one swift move, ripped them from her body.

"Lean back," he told her, as his hands went to the back of her thighs and he lifted her legs to his shoulders.

At that moment, she was thankful that she kept her desk neat. Myles had his face buried in her pussy before her back hit the wooden surface.

"Oh my damnnn!" she shrieked.

He sucked her clit hard before he let his tongue slither between her lips. Using his fingers, he separated them to give his mouth better access. Dipping his tongue inside her drenched hole, he lapped up the juices that were freely flowing, causing her only to release more juices. The flavor of her nectar was so delicious, putting him in the mind of sweet cream.

"Baabbyy, this feels so fucking good."

His thumb went to massage her protruding nub while his index and middle fingers slid inside her slippery center. His tongue managed not to miss a beat, bringing her to the height of her climax.

"Fuuccccckkk, baby, I'm cummin'!"

Myles didn't let up as Everleigh's hands went to the back of his head, pulling him closer, and her legs clamped around his neck. The dam between her thighs broke, soaking his face with her sweet honey. When he finally came up for air, he wasted no time standing, pushing his sweats and underwear down, and plunging deep inside Everleigh's haven.

"Argh!" he groaned when her walls wrapped tightly around his dick.

"Fuck me, baby. Beat this pussy up!"

No further encouragement was needed. Myles pounded deep into Everleigh's pussy. All that could be heard was the sound of his balls slapping her ass cheeks and their moans and groans of ecstasy. Only minutes later, he could feel her pussy pulsing around him. Any other time, he would have slowed his strokes to prolong the session. This time, he let her walls rob him of his seeds and collapsed on top of her, completely satisfied.

CHAPTER 22

While Everleigh took care of business in L.A., Myles did the same in Seattle. The first order of business was to talk to Mr. Everette. Luckily, he was an early riser, and Myles was able to see him before he went to his shop. After ringing the doorbell, he waited patiently for Mr. Everette to answer the door.

"One of these days, I'm gonna leave you out here. Use your key, son," he fussed.

"Yessir, if you insist," Myles replied as he followed him to the kitchen.

"Hell, yeah, I insist. You practically been living here since Ev's been back."

"Does that bother you, Mr. Everette? Am I here too much?"

"Myles, you're like a son to me. I don't care nothing about how much you visit. It would be nice if you and Ev could save that wild sex for when she's at your place, though."

Myles looked at him with a shocked expression but still managed to a smirk.

"Damn! I ain't think you could hear us. My bad."

"Don't worry about it. Hopefully, I'll get a grandchild soon. Now, what brings you by so early?"

"I wanted to talk to you about something. Can we sit?"

"How about you sit? I was just about to make my coffee."

Myles sat at the kitchen table while Mr. Everette prepared his morning coffee. For some reason, Myles had become very nervous. However, he had to do this so that he could move forward with the rest of his plans.

"I wanna marry Leigh...as soon as possible. I came to get your blessing."

Mr. Everette turned to face Myles and looked at him with a broad smile.

"Without a doubt. You've always had me and Dinah's blessing."

"Thank you, and I don't take that lightly. I can't thank you enough for the influence you had and continue to have on me. What I can do is promise to love, honor, and cherish your daughter until the day I take my last breath."

"That's all I ask."

He sat down in the chair across from Myles and sipped his coffee.

"Can I be straight up for a minute?"

"Always, son."

"At first, when Leigh started gettin' on me about the streets, I ain't like that shit. She knew what I was into when we got together. Even when one of my boys got locked up, and another one got killed, I still couldn't see myself walking away. Then I almost got shot...the bullet just missed my head. I never told Leigh about that, but that was when I started to make some moves to walk away. The thought of how devastated she would have been if I'd been killed did something to me. Mr. Everette, I was literally days away from leaving all that shit behind. I had one more big shipment coming in, and I was done. But she left."

"I know none of it matters now, but you still could have walked away."

"I could have, but I was so pissed at her, and I took my anger right to the streets."

"You were hurt," he added.

"I didn't want to admit it at the time, but yeah, I was hurt. Honestly, it broke me. Once she was gone, I ain't wanna think or feel, so instead of leaving, I got in deeper. I told Leigh that the only reason I'm still here, living and breathing, with no bullet wounds, and my freedom, is because of God, and the prayers of my family and hers."

"God spared you for a reason. Now, it's up to you to find out what that reason is."

Myles stood and reached in the pocket of his sweats, pulling out a little black box.

"I know one of them is to make Leigh my wife. I bought this ring over twelve years ago before she left. I could never bring myself to do anything with it."

Mr. Everette took the box from Myles and got a closer look at the ring. He wore a satisfied smile as he nodded his head in approval.

"Well, it doesn't look twelve years old. She'll love it. How do you plan to propose?"

"I've been thinking about that, and I have an idea I wanna run by you."

"Let me hear it."

ABOUT AN HOUR LATER, MYLES WAS ABOUT TO GET STARTED ON the first car of the day, when he felt someone's presence. He turned around and saw Jory standing just outside the garage.

"Wassup, bruh. You sneaking up on mugs now?"

"Naw, I ain't see you at first, and I was just looking around."

Myles wasn't sure why Jory's whole vibe seemed off the last couple times he'd seen him, but something was definitely up.

"You good?"

"I'm straight. I came by a couple days ago, but you were closed."

"Yeah, I had to go out to L.A. right quick and take care of something with Leigh."

"She good?"

"She is now. She's still out there packin' up her shit to move back."

"Word? So, she's for sure moving back. You sure you ready to be on lockdown again."

"If it's with her, hell yeah."

"I still say you a better man than me. But umm, I came to see if you gave any thought to that favor I asked. You know I wouldn't even put you in this position if I ain't have to."

"Real talk, I ain't had time to think about it. The day after we talked, I had to catch a red-eye to L.A. Shit was kinda hectic for a few days; then it slipped my mind."

"Damn, bruh! It ain't nothin' to think about. Either you gon' do it or you not."

Myles's face went into a frown from Jory's tone and attitude.

"Nigga, who the fuck you talkin' to?"

"My bad, bruh. Options are slim, and if you can't do it, I need to find somewhere else."

"Gon' head and do that shit then, nigga. 'Cause I can't help you."

"You can't or you won't?"

"Both nigga. I'll holla."

Myles got back to work as if Jory was never there, but Jory didn't leave right away. He couldn't leave without saying one last thing.

"I meant to ask you before, but it slipped my mind," Jory said.

Myles stopped what he was doing and gave him his attention again.

"What?"

"You haven't said anything about a kid, so I'm guessing she got rid of it."

"She who?"

"Ev."

"The hell are you talkin' about, bruh?"

"Oh, shit, my bad. You ain't know? You might wanna have a conversation with ya girl. It ain't my place to say."

With that, Jory disappeared around the building, leaving Myles dumbfounded and speechless. He pulled out his phone to call Everleigh but thought better of it. She would never keep something as significant as a pregnancy, or baby, from him. He put his phone back in this pocket, deciding that Jory had to be lying. *How would he know something like that, anyway?*

CHAPTER 23

Everleigh had been back from L.A. for a few hours. The chaos of moving her things had her ready to pull all her hair out. She had no idea how she accumulated so many clothes and shoes, especially because she didn't enjoy shopping. Instead of using the Briggs' company jet, Myles hired a moving company. She was grateful because they also took care of the shipping of her car, and that helped expedite the process. The room she had at her parent's house wasn't nearly enough space, so she ended up putting her winter and most of her fall clothing in storage.

The last few days that she was in L.A., Myles seemed very distant. Instead of multiple FaceTime calls each day, they spoke only once a day, and it wasn't on FaceTime. She initiated the text messages between the two, and he replied with one word or very short answers. He'd been so distant that it surprised her that he'd hired movers and paid for a storage unit for her.

After spending a few hours with her father, Everleigh was anxious to see her man, so she packed a duffle bag to spend a couple days at Myles's place. She still didn't like leaving her father alone, but after being in L.A. longer than she planned, she realized that he handled being alone just fine. Going to therapy was helping him a great deal, and she was thankful that he'd been open to it.

Before leaving, she made her dad's favorite meal, which was smothered pork chops, mashed potatoes, green beans, and cornbread. After he blessed the food, her father shared some news with her.

"I got a phone call from the corporate office of the Boys and Girls Club."

"Really? What'd they say?" Everleigh answered as if she didn't know the reason for their call.

"Apparently, a donation for a million dollars was donated in your mother's name...anonymously. "

"Wow! That's awesome! I wonder who would do something so grand in honor of Ma."

He put his fork down and looked at her with squinted eyes.

"The only person we know that has that kinda money is that fool, Easton. Did you have something to do with this?"

Still pretending to be clueless, she replied, "What makes you think I had something to do with it? Maybe he felt—"

"Cut the crap, Ev," he interrupted her, and she fell into a fit of laughter.

"Okay, Daddy. I did know about it, but I had nothing to do with it. It was all Myles."

"Myles?"

She nodded as she finished chewing a forkful of food. "You know Myles came to L.A. with one thing on his mind. Fortunately, God interceded, and it didn't happen. I mean, he did break Easton's nose, but it could've been much worse. Myles made him agree to donate one million dollars to the club within the week, followed by five hundred thousand a year for the next five years."

"He negotiated all that?" he asked.

"Well, I wouldn't say he negotiated." She laughed. "If Easton refused, he threatened to post the pics of my bruised face on social media."

"That sounds more like Myles."

"He's so amazing, Daddy. Ma would be pleased."

"She sure would be. The man on the phone said they'd be doing some renovations to all of the locations in Seattle, and there will be a section named in honor of your mother at each one."

"Really? Now that, I didn't know. That's amazing!"

"It is. Myles is a good man, Ev. He always has been."

"I know, Daddy."

"Now that you're back, what are you gonna do with that fancy studio in L.A.?" he asked.

"My lease is up in six months. I'll keep it until then."

After having dinner, she made a plate to take to Myles, cleaned up the kitchen, and was on her way. He'd given her a key before she went to L.A.; however, he pulled the door open before she could use it.

"Anxious much?" she teased.

"Naw, but I'm hungry as hell. I ain't know you was gon' be that long, baby."

He stepped to the side to give her room to enter. Once she was inside, he closed and locked the door, then kissed her forehead before taking the plate from her hands and heading to the kitchen. Everleigh slipped off her shoes and took her bag and purse to his bedroom. By the time she returned, he was sitting at the breakfast bar feeding his face, so she slid onto the stool next to him.

"I'm sorry it took so long. I didn't plan to eat with daddy, but I was hungry."

Myles paused with his fork midway to his mouth and looked at her.

"Ya think?" He shook his head and went back to eating.

"Whatever! Just be happy you got your damn food."

"I am happy. This shit good as hell, too, baby." He leaned over with his mouth full and pecked her cheek. "I appreciate you hooking me up."

"Of course. So...I was talking to Daddy while we ate. He said someone from the Boys & Girls Club called him. Looks like Easton held up his end of the bargain."

"That nigga ain't crazy. He ain't have a choice," he said between bites.

"His reputation is way too important to him to risk being seen as an abuser. Daddy says they're renovating all the locations here and are gonna name a section after Ma. Was that part of your plan?"

"Maybe," he said with a smirk and a wink.

Everleigh took that as a yes and planned on thanking him in the best possible way, once they went to bed.

"Slow down, baby. You're inhaling that food."

"I told you I was hungry. I worked through lunch to finish a couple limos. I'm grateful for this new contract, but I gon' have to hire somebody full-time."

Everleigh observed Myles's demeanor and recalled his reception of her when she arrived. He didn't seem distant and was acting normal. It's always hard to decipher someone's mood through text messages. He'd also been busy at his shop, so she figured him being tired and could have contributed to their lack of communication.

"Have you had the boys from the club start yet?"

"Not until next week. That'll help, but once school starts, they can only work weekends."

"Baby, I know you aren't into social media, and I understand why, considering your former lifestyle, but you should strongly consider at least creating an Instagram for MAAD."

"You know I don't know nothin' about that shit."

"I know, but you need to learn. These days, businesses can't be successful without social media."

"I disagree, baby. Weren't we just talkin' about me needin' some help because business is so good?"

"That's true, and it's kind of amazing considering you don't use social media in any way. How about this? I'll create a page and manage it for you until you learn how to do it. The first post we make will be about the position you're looking to fill. Sound good?"

He shrugged his shoulders as he cleaned his plate. "Go for it."

"Oooh, and tomorrow, I can come by and take some pictures of the building and you working. We can post those, too."

"Whatever you wanna do is fine."

"What about a website? Do you have a website? I can probably—"

"Slow down, Leigh. One thing at a time. Let's start with the Instagram page."

She sighed. "Okay, fine. Where's your phone so I can download the app and create your account?"

"On the table in the living room," he told her as he went to the sink to wash his plate.

"What's the—"

"Your birthday."

She looked in his direction, but his back was facing her. By the time she was standing next to him, he was done washing his plate and reaching for a napkin to dry his hands.

"The code is my birthday?"

"Yeah? Why you sound surprised?"

Instead of answering, she went to her purse to retrieve her phone. When she returned, Myles was leaning against the counter.

"Here." She handed him her phone, and he gave her a strange look. "Put the code in...it's your birthday."

"No shit?"

When they both had successfully unlocked each other's phones, their eyes met, and their lips curled into a smile. He placed her phone on the counter, wrapped his arms around her, then kissed her lips.

"You're mine. Always have been, always will be," he said.

"I know."

They shared another kiss before moving to the living room and getting comfortable on the couch. Myles sat down first, extending his body the entire length, and Everleigh sat between his legs, with her back against his chest. She held his phone in a position that they could both see the screen as she downloaded the Instagram app and began the steps to creating his account. Once it was set up, she showed him the basics, like how to post pictures and videos, and follow and unfollow people.

"See, it's not that bad," she said.

"Don't seem like it."

He took his phone and put it on the coffee table, then wrapped his arms around her, resting his hands on her stomach, and his chin on top of her head. Everleigh felt his mood shift and waited for him to say something. For a good five minutes, they sat in silence.

Myles was trying to stay out of his head. He'd been thinking about what Jory said since the words left his mouth. Although he was able to talk himself out of asking her about it while she was still in L.A., it plagued his mind. Now that they're in each other's presence again, he's having a hard time not bringing it up.

"How does it feel to be officially back?" he finally said.

"Fine. Seattle has always been home for me. It's not like I haven't been visiting."

"How often did you visit?"

"Every other month."

"Even when you first left? I remember when I started havin' dinner with your parents, they would complain about you not visiting.'

"Oh, yeah. That first year, I didn't come home at all. I was... trying to get settled. But after that year, I was here every other month. I can't believe we never saw each other."

He felt her body tense when she mentioned the first year she was away. Myles began to connect some dots that he prayed wouldn't connect.

"We weren't meant to see each other again, until the moment we did. God has a way of workin' shit out exactly how it's supposed to be."

"You think?"

"I know. I stopped questioning Him a long time ago."

The tone of his voice made Everleigh shiver. *Something was definitely off with him, she thought.* Turning around to face him, she folded her arms across his chest and rested her chin on them. This position put them face-to-face.

"Is there something wrong?" she asked.

"What makes you think something's wrong?"

"I don't know, nothing specific. I felt like you were kind of distant the last few days I was gone. When I got here, you seemed cool, but even now, I feel like you're somewhere else."

He shook his head. "Let's talk. Twelve years is a long time. I bet there's some shit about you I don't know."

Since they'd been back together, they'd spent countless hours reminiscing and catching up. Everleigh didn't feel like there was much that she hadn't told him about their time apart, but if he wanted to talk, she had no problem with it.

"Okay. What do you think you don't know?"

"Were you pregnant when you left?" He couldn't fight it a second longer. He had to know.

Her stomach lurched, and she could feel herself starting to sweat. She tried to lift her body from his, but his arms were wrapped around her, stopping her from moving.

"What are you talking about?" she said as calmly as she could.

"Answer the question. Look me in my eyes and tell me if you were pregnant when you ran off to L.A."

She couldn't look him in his eyes because then she'd be forced to tell him the truth, and she didn't want him to know the truth. Nobody knew, not even her parents.

"Can you let me up, please?"

He removed his arms from around her body, and she pushed up and away from him as quickly as she could. When she tried to get off the couch, he grabbed her by the arm and held her in place.

"Leigh..."

Tears blurred her vision and wet her face. Using her hands to cover her face, she began to cry uncontrollably. Myles didn't press her anymore for the answer because her reaction said it all. He now had other questions.

"What happened to my baby, Leigh?"

She shook her head back and forth, hoping that his questions would stop, or that she'd vanish into thin air.

"Myles, please. I'm sorry I didn't tell you, but I can't talk about this. Please, don't make me talk about this."

"Was it my baby?"

The question cut her to her core. She flung her head in his direction and glared at him in disbelief.

"How could you ask me that? Up until years after I left, you were the only man I'd ever been with."

Shooting up off the couch, she headed for the door. Again, Myles caught her before she was out of his reach and pulled her down to his lap. He used one arm to keep her in place, and his free hand went to grip her chin and turn her face to his.

"I asked you because I don't fuckin' know. If it was my baby, I should already know. If it wasn't, that's some shit I need to know, too. Now, answer my damn question!"

"Yes, okay! Yes, I was pregnant, and he was yours!" she shouted in his face. "You happy now!"

Everleigh did her best to remove herself from his grip but to no avail.

"No! I'm not fuckin' happy. Why didn't you tell me? Where's the fuck is my son, Leigh? What the fuck did you do with my son?"

"I didn't do anything," she cried. "I did everything right, and he died, Myles. He was stillborn!"

Her head fell into his chest as she bawled her eyes out. While Myles processed her words, his arms wrapped tightly around her, and he rubbed her back. *Stillborn? His son is dead?* A single tear fell from his eye as his mind went to the night their bodies reunited. He recalled the fullness of her hips and ass, the thickness of her thighs, her plump breasts, and her stretch marks. All he could think was that his son did that to her, and he wasn't there to witness any of it because she stole that experience from him. He wanted to console her and mourn the son he never knew he had, but his heart was broken, and he was angry...and he still had a question.

"How did Jory know?" he asked as calmly as he could.

This day could not get any worse for Everleigh. Myles just kept gut-punching her.

"Know what?" she asked, playing dumb.

"How the fuck did he know you were pregnant?"

"I, umm, I don't know how he would know. I didn't tell anyone."

"You lyin' to me, Leigh, and until you can be honest about all this shit, I'm gon' need a minute."

He pushed her off his lap, and she landed next to him on the couch.

"What do you mean?" she asked, as he stood and walked toward the back of the townhome but stopped to address her question.

"Exactly what I said. You hid something so important from me, a whole kid, for all these years. I can't even properly mourn my own fuckin' son because I didn't know about him until two minutes ago. If it wasn't for Jory, I still wouldn't know. You gotta go!"

He continued his trek to his bedroom and got her purse and duffle bag, then went to the kitchen to get her phone from the counter. Everleigh remained seated on the couch with her arms wrapped around her torso, and tears falling from her eyes. She felt nauseous and lightheaded. Myles pulled her to her feet and shoved her belonging into her arms. He was doing his best not to be too rough with her as he guided her to the door. He didn't speak again until she was outside.

"I need some time."

Everleigh didn't have the energy nor desire to fight with him. If he felt like he needed some time, she'd give him some time. She turned to go to her car, and when she was a few steps away, she turned to face him one more time.

"I love you, Myles, and I'm sorry I keep hurting you."

Without a response, he closed the door, delivering yet another gut punch. *He didn't even make sure I got to my car safely.*

WHEN EVERLEIGH LEFT, HE NEEDED TO TALK TO SOMEBODY, SO HE called his mother. They hadn't been talking as often as they usually did because his time had been limited between work and Everleigh.

"Is this my son?" Delilah answered. Myles should have been prepared for her to fuss at him.

"Yeah, Ma, it's me."

"Are you okay? You don't sound right."

"I had a son, Ma."

"Wait a damn minute. I know damn well you ain't get some lil—"

"Naw, Ma, I didn't. Just listen for a minute, please."

"Okay, I'm listening."

"Everleigh gave birth to my son. She was pregnant when she moved to L.A."

"Nooo! That can't be true. She kept him from you all this time?"

"He was stillborn, Ma. So, naw, she ain't keep him from me, per se, but I just now found out about him."

Delilah gasped, and her eyes immediately began to water.

"Son, that's terrible. I'm so sorry. What happened? Why didn't she tell you?"

"I don't know the details. Once she finally fessed up, I needed a minute."

"Myles, listen, son. I know right now you're upset and probably have all kinds of bad thoughts in your head about Everleigh. Before you jump to any conclusions, hear her out. If she kept something like that from you, there had to be a legitimate reason."

"I can't think of a reason good enough. I gotta go, Ma. I'll hit you later."

"Okay, Myles, but don't forget what I said. Hear her out."

"Love you, Ma."

"Love you, too."

Myles went to his room and fell back on his bed. An hour later, he was still in the same position, staring at the ceiling. He replayed the conversation with Everleigh over and over, hoping that he misunderstood something.

While she was in L.A., he promised himself that he would not address what Jory told him with her. He was confident that she would never keep such a secret. As hard as he tried to put it out of his mind, the more it remained at the forefront. Everleigh definitely wasn't imagining the distance she felt.

Myles was having a hard time processing that she carried his baby and watched him grow for nine months in her belly, only to lose him. Not only that but that she went through all of it alone. The reality of that hit him, and he realized that he was too hard on her. He let his anger and hurt control his reaction. *Why would she go through that alone when she didn't have to?* Something wasn't adding up, and his gut was telling him that Jory might have some answers.

Hopping out of bed, he pulled on a hoodie and grabbed his keys and phone. As he was putting on his shoes, which were near the front door, there was a knock on the door. He pulled it open without asking who it was. Seeing Mr. Everette there, surprised him. It was necessary to ask the reason for his visit, so he stepped to the side and welcomed him in.

"I'm sure you know why I'm here."

"I think so."

"Good, so you can you tell me why my daughter left my house happier than a pig in shit and came home with puffy eyes and snot all over her face. What the hell happened?"

"Can we sit?"

Mr. Everette nodded then followed Myles to his living room.

"Did she tell you anything?"

"No. I happened to be leaving the kitchen when she came in, and I saw her face. When she saw me, she ran to her room, then slammed and locked the door. I could hear her sobbing, and I tried to get her to open up and let me in, but she told me to go away."

Releasing a deep sigh, Myles rubbed his hand down his face.

"Let me apologize for my language right now."

"Don't worry about it, son. Speak your mind."

"I honestly don't know where to begin or how to say this. It may not even be my place to say, but I'm gon' take the liberty and tell you anyway."

"Spill it!"

"Leigh was pregnant when she moved to L.A. Apparently, she didn't tell anyone."

"Pregnant? What—where's the child? Did she—"

"She told me it was stillborn."

There was confusion written all over Mr. Everette's face, and Myles understood completely because he was confused as well.

"Stillborn? My God. Why would she hide something like that? It makes no sense."

"Been trying to figure that out for the last hour. When she finally told me the truth, I ain't handle it well, but I couldn't be around her. I love Leigh, more than anything in this world, but the hurt she's caused me..." He shook his head as he tried to find the right words. "I've killed niggas for less. I had to pull the truth outta her and she still ain't told me everything. How can I marry her, knowing that she can't be all the way real with me?"

Mr. Everette didn't respond right away. For the life of him, he couldn't understand why Everleigh would up and move away, knowing she was pregnant, and not tell anyone.

"Maybe Dinah knew."

Myles shook his head. "Naw, Ms. Dinah ain't know. Leigh said nobody knew."

"How did you find out?"

That question brought Myles's mind back to where he was about to go.

"My boy, Jory. He came by the shop a few days ago, and as he was leaving, he asked me how I was able to forgive Leigh for getting rid of my kid."

"Who is this...Jory? Does he talk to Ev? Are they friends, as well?"

"She ain't never liked Jory. I think she hated him, honestly. Which is why I'm messed up about him knowin' some shit about my woman that I ain't know, and it don't seem like she was plannin' to tell me."

"This is making less and less sense," Mr. Everette said.

Myles nodded in agreement. "I was about to go find out what Jory knows when you showed up."

Now it was Mr. Everette's turn to shake his head. "Why would you talk to him when Ev has all the information you need? Look, son, you have every right to be upset with her. Hell, I'm upset, too. But before you talk to anybody else about a situation that only concerns the two of you, you need to talk to her."

"I want answers right now, but I can't talk to her...not yet."

"Well, you wait. This Jory character probably don't mean you no good anyway. If he's known about this all this time and didn't say a word, what's his motive for telling you now?"

Myles thought about what he said and agreed that he did have a point. He hadn't had a good feeling about Jory the last few times they were in the same space, anyway. He decided to hold off on having a conversation with him...for now.

"You right, I should talk to Leigh, but I don't know when. What she did was wrong as hell, and if I talk to her now, I'm gon' make this shit worse than it is."

"I understand, son."

Mr. Everette stood to leave, and Myles walked him to the door. Nothing else was said because there was nothing else to say.

CHAPTER 24

After staying locked away in her room for five days, barely eating, sleeping, or talking to her father, Everleigh finally decided that she couldn't put off bathing any longer. She took a much-needed shower, washing her hair as well, and after dressing in a pair of sweats and a long-sleeved t-shirt, she left the confines of her room.

The house was quiet, so she thought that her father wasn't home. After making herself two slices of toast and spreading some butter on them, she grabbed a bottle of water from the fridge and took a seat at the kitchen table. That's all she'd been eating since the morning after Myles told her to leave his place.

Between crying spells, she'd done a lot of thinking and concluded that she had no choice. She had to leave Seattle to keep the people that she loved safe. There was no way around it. Even though it seemed as if all her decisions were coming back to bite her in the ass, she would do it all over again if it meant no harm would come to them.

She couldn't believe how quickly things between her and Myles had changed. He was understandably angry and hurt, but she'd been praying for the past five days that he would find it in his heart to forgive her. Hurting him had never been her intention, protecting him was.

Finishing up her toast, she took the bottle of water and went to the family room. Just as she sat in the corner of the couch, she heard the front door open and close, then her father entered. She looked everywhere, but in his eyes, and after a few long seconds, he sat down next to her on the couch.

"You finally decided to wash your ass and come outta that room, huh?"

"Daddy, please. Not right now."

"If not now, when, baby girl. I left you alone for damn near a week. You need to tell me what's wrong."

As if on cue, tears filled her eyes. "Everything is wrong, Daddy. Everything."

She covered her face and cried into her hands as her father put his arm around her should and pulled her into his side.

"You should know that I talked to Myles, and he told me everything he knew."

Lifting her head slowly, her eyes finally met those of her father.

"So...you know?"

He reached for her, and she "Yes, baby girl, I know. Why didn't you tell us? It breaks my heart that you went through something so tragic all alone. Your mother would be devastated."

"I would have told you, eventually. I just...I didn't tell you before I left because I didn't want you to try to convince me to stay. I *had* to leave, Daddy. Once the baby didn't make it, I didn't see the point in telling everyone something so sad."

"Why did you feel like moving was your only option? I understand you had your reasons for ending things with Myles, but you could have always come back home."

She shook her head as she said, "No, I couldn't. I had to leave town. It was the only way to guarantee..."

When she realized she was about to say too much, she stopped herself.

"To guarantee what, Ev?"

"I can't."

Before he could stop her, she hopped up from the couch and ran back to her bedroom, locking herself inside. If she tells her father why she really left town, he's going to tell Myles, and that's gonna open up a can of worms that needs to remain closed. Tossing herself on her bed, she cried herself sick, and almost didn't make it to the bathroom in time. All she could do was dry heave because her stomach was so empty.

In the family room, Mr. Everette was fed up with the nonsense. It was like his daughter, who he thought could talk to him and his wife about everything, had been leading some kind of double life. After Everleigh locked herself in her room, he called Myles.

"Everything good, Mr. Everette."

"You know damn well it's not. Something is going on with Ev, and I need to get to the bottom of it. You need to get outta your feelings and find out why she did what she did. She's not talking to me, but I know my daughter, and she wouldn't do nothing like that unless she felt she had to. You say you love her, well act like it. Dammit!"

He ended the call before Myles could respond. On the other side of town, Myles looked at his phone. He'd never heard Mr. Everette so angry. He could also detect a little worry in his voice. It had been five days since he'd last seen or talked to him and Everleigh. Every time he thought he might be ready, his heart told him he needed more time. He knew that whatever it was that Everleigh was keeping from him, would change everything between them. He wasn't sure if he was ready for that and what it could mean.

LATER ON THAT NIGHT, MYLES WAS IN FRONT OF THE NOBLE residence, sitting in his truck, debating on whether or not he should go in. Mr. Everette saw him when he pulled up and had been waiting for him to ring the doorbell. After fifteen minutes, he stepped out on his porch and yelled at him.

"Son, don't make me go get my gun," was all he said before going back inside.

Myles shook his head and laughed at the thought of Mr. Everette pulling a gun on him. He believed he would do it, though. He left the door open, and once inside, Myles locked up. As he was about to go to the family room, he heard Mr. Everette say, "She's in her room. The key is on the top of the doorframe."

Changing directions, he headed to Everleigh's room and retrieved the key, before slowly letting himself inside. The room was dark, aside from the light that was coming from the bathroom because the door was partially open. She wasn't in bed, so he assumed that's where she was. He slowly closed the bedroom door and leaned against it as he waited for her to step out of the bathroom. Seconds later, the bathroom light turned off, and she came out, going straight to the bed and burying herself under the comforter.

Myles walked softly across the room and sat in the sofa chair in the corner of the room as he did a couple months ago. After making himself comfortable, he called her name.

"Leigh," he said softly, not wanting to startle her.

Since she had no idea he was in the room, he scared almost scared her to death.

"Shit!" she shouted as her body jolted up. "You trying to give me a heart attack?"

He didn't respond. She sat up and turned on the lamp that was on the side of the bed, then put her back against the headboard.

"It's past time for you to be honest with me. As much as I love you and you say you love me, if you can't do that, our love don't mean shit. I want you to start from the beginning and don't leave a damn thing out."

CHAPTER 25

Everleigh closed her eyes and took a deep breath. If she could have it her way, she'd never talk about this situation ever again. Jory got what he wanted, so she didn't understand why he was still trying to ruin her life. She never confirmed that she was pregnant when Jory asked her, all those years ago. It was clear that he intended to stir up drama between her and Myles.

"One night," she began. "When I came home from my night class, Jory approached me."

"Approached you where?"

"In our parking garage," she replied.

"Jory was in our parking garage?"

"Yes. He didn't like that I wanted you to stop hustling and..."

She went on to tell him about the conversation in the garage, and the one that occurred at her school. Myles kept shifting in his seat, cracking his knuckles, and releasing deep breaths. He was visibly upset but didn't speak until it seemed as if she was done talking.

"Why you ain't come to me the first time he stepped to you, Leigh? I would have ended his ass on sight."

"I was scared," she confessed as tears poured from her eyes. "More like terrified. You know I've always thought Jory was evil.

That last straw was when I found out I was pregnant. I was gonna tell you everything that night, but when I left the doctor's office, Jory was waiting by my car. He threatened my parents again and said that if he didn't kill you, he'd have you set up and doing life. Then he said while you were locked up—while you were locked up, or dead, he—I would be his, and your baby would be calling him daddy."

He jumped up from the chair and shouted, "And you ain't tell me this shit. I can't believe you, Leigh. How could you let that nigga force you away from your family and not say a fuckin' word? You ain't think I could protect you?"

"You know how green and naïve I was back then," she shouted back. "I didn't—"

"Fuuuccckkk!" he roared from deep within his soul. Everleigh swore she felt the whole room shake. "That's why you shoulda came to me! That nigga took away twelve years of my life, Leigh. I lost you for twelve-fuckin-years. I lost the chance to be excited about havin' a baby with the only woman I've ever loved. I lost the chance to be excited about having a boy. I lost the chance to watch my son grow inside you. I lost the chance to have hopes and dreams for him. I lost the chance to show him I loved him before he was laid to rest. I fuckin' lost the chance to mourn my son. I lost all that because you were too afraid to tell me what his bitch ass was doing."

Myles was out of breath, sweating, and well past angry. In his entire life, he'd never felt the kind of hurt he felt at that moment. Not even when Everleigh left him. He felt betrayed, not just by Jory, but by Everleigh. All these years, he thought he was the cause of her leaving. To know that she didn't trust him enough to protect them and confide in him that their lives were being threatened, made him feel some kind of way...and it didn't feel good.

She crawled to the foot and got out, reaching for Myles.

"Don't touch me," he barked, moving out of her reach.

"I'm sorry," she wailed. "I'm so sorry, baby, please. You have to forgive me."

"I ain't gotta do shit right now. I'm out!"

He pulled the door to her bedroom so aggressively that it slammed hard against the back wall and swung back to the closed position. Seconds later, when she heard the front door slam, she fell to her knees and cried until her tears dried up. Her father had come in and tried to get her off the floor, but she didn't want to move. He managed to get his old body down on the floor with her and pulled her head into his lap, consoling her as much as he could.

When Myles got into his car, he was ready to explode. So many emotions were bottled up inside him, and he didn't know how to express them. He fought it until he couldn't fight anymore. The tears won the battle and poured from his eyes. He cried for the years that he'd lost with his love; he cried for the loss of the son that their love created, and the pain of knowing the truth.

Looking up at the house, he felt bad for walking out the way he did and how he'd been treating the woman he loved more than life. She was the only woman that could get him so deep in his feelings. There was no question about whether or not he would forgive her because he refused to do life without her. But first, some things needed to be taken care of.

Myles left the Noble residence on a mission. He already knew what had to be done, and this time, not a soul on earth could talk him out of it. Lucky for him, before going to see Everleigh, he pulled up on Jory at one of the spots he was familiar with from his hustling days. Myles already knew that whatever Everleigh told him, Jory was somehow involved. Of course, he didn't know to what extent at the time, but that didn't matter. He knew that after he found out Jory's level of involvement, at a minimum, he would have to beat his ass.

Myles could see the surprised look on Jory's face when he walked in. He could tell that Jory was nervous but was trying to play it off.

"Wassup?" Jory said, focusing on his phone.

"Leigh ain't who I thought she was, bruh."

"Word? Why you say that?"

"I confronted her about being pregnant. I had to pull it out of her, but she finally admitted the shit. She got an abortion and ain't plan on telling a nigga."

"These bitches be out here living foul as hell. I'm glad I could enlighten you, man," Jory said, proudly.

"How did you know? I was so pissed, I forgot to tell her how I found out."

"Oh, shit. I, umm, the girl I was fuckin' with at the time, thought she was pregnant. I went to the doctor with her and saw Ev there."

"It's fucked up you ain't say shit then, but I get it, it wasn't your place."

"Naw, I ain't think it was. We cool?" Jory asked, extending his fist for a pound.

"Always, bruh. If it wasn't for you, I would have married a lie," Myles replied, connecting his fist with Jory's.

Now that Myles knew that Jory was the catalyst behind him losing so much, he had to pay the ultimate price.

CHAPTER 26

Myles pulled his truck into the garage of MAAD. After changing into one of his work shirts, he got everything he needed to start detailing his truck. Once his phone connected to the Bluetooth speaker, he chose an old school hip hop playlist on Spotify and got to work.

About twenty minutes later, he heard a noise at the back entrance of the garage. Before he started on his truck, he'd gone to the storage shed he had out back and didn't lock the door when he came back in. Grabbing his .357, he waited behind his truck. Because of the music, Myles couldn't hear any movement, but his street sense made him aware of someone's presence.

The light in the garage was on, allowing him to see the shadow of the intruder. As soon as the shadow got close enough, Myles stepped from behind his truck, slammed the intruder against the side, then put his gun to his head.

"Fuck, bruh!" Jory said, putting his hands up against the truck.

"The fuck you doin' here?"

"I was driving by and saw the lights on," Jory explained.

"Ain't shit around here for you to be driving by at this time!" He pressed the gun harder into Jory's head.

"Damn, man! Chill! You said earlier you'd be here cleaning your truck. I thought since we squashed all that shit from a few days ago, you might reconsider doing me that favor."

"So fuckin' predictable. You did exactly what I thought you would."

"What?"

"Ain't shit squashed. I told you I was gon' be here 'cause I knew you'd show up. Leigh told me what yo' bitch ass did."

"Man, that hoe—"

Myles hit him on the side of his face with the butt of the gun and pulled his body away from the truck. Jory was stunned momentarily, causing him to stumble, but he didn't fall. Myles knew Jory was strapped because that's how they moved, so he was prepared when Jory reached for his gun. Before Jory could get a good grip, Myles fired off a shot. The bullet hit Jory's shoulder, causing him to fall to the ground, groaning loudly, and dropped his gun. If Myles didn't need it to look like self-defense, Jory would already be dead.

"All this, over a bitch that ain't even loyal to you," Jory spat.

"Fuck you know about loyalty, nigga? All that sneak shit you did, and you wanna talk about loyalty?"

"Naw, I'd rather talk about how yo' bitch mouth felt around my dick."

Jory picked up his gun, which had fallen right next to his knee, and pulled the trigger. The bullet grazed Myles's shoulder. At the exact same time, Myles fired off another shot, hitting Jory in the chest. Almost immediately, Jory collapsed.

❦

THE FOLLOWING MORNING, EVERLEIGH WOKE UP WITH A pounding headache. When the memories of the night before came rushing back, she was sure tears would follow, but to her surprise, there were none. Everleigh was all cried out.

After taking care of her hygiene, she dressed in a pair of denim shorts and a tank top. When she left her room, she found her father in his recliner in the family room. Their eyes connected, and she sensed that there was something different about him. She'd been so caught up in her mess of a life for the past week, she forgot that her father was in mourning.

"You okay, Daddy?"

"I'm fine? How are you?"

"I'm not fine, but I will be. There's something different about you. You sure you okay?"

"Yes, baby girl, I'm okay. I slept in the bedroom for the first time last night."

Her eyes got wide with surprise. "Oh, wow, Daddy. Did you sleep okay?"

He nodded with a smile. "Not at first. I'm not even sure what made me stay in there last night after my shower. When I first laid down, I was so worried about you and this situation with Myles. My mind was everywhere, but eventually, I dozed off and guess what. Your mother came to me."

With her eyes even wider, she said, "Really? What'd she say?"

"Before or after she fussed at me for sleeping in this chair for the past three months."

They shared a laugh. It wouldn't be Dinah if she didn't fuss at him about something.

"After," Everleigh replied.

"She told me that she's at peace, that we shouldn't worry about her, and that everything with you and Myles would work itself out."

Releasing a deep sigh, she said, "I've always felt that Mommy was at peace. Maybe that's why I was able to move forward as quickly as I did. I miss her so much, and I wish I could tell her about everything I've been through. I can only imagine what she would say."

That sat quietly for a few minutes, each of them thinking about the woman they loved and missed a great deal. The television suddenly captured their attention when they noticed MAAD on the screen.

"Daddy, turn it up."

"Apparently, the owner, Mr. Myles Abbott, had come to his shop, Myles

Abbott Auto Detailing, also known as MAAD, after hours to clean and detail his own vehicle. The intruder, Mr. Jory Stone, tried to rob Mr. Abbott at gunpoint. Both men were shot, and unfortunately, Mr. Stone didn't make it. Mr. Abbott was taken to UW Medical Center and will make a full recovery. This is Joan Hantler, reporting for King-5 News."

"Oh my God, Daddy, Myles was shot."

Everleigh frantically ran to her room to get her phone and Face-timed Myles. When he didn't answer, her heart dropped. Although the lady on the news said that he was expected to make a full recovery, that didn't give her much information. *Where was he shot? Did he need surgery? Is he still in the hospital?* Everleigh had questions, and she needed answers. Before she completely panicked, she called the hospital.

"Hello! Can you connect me to the room of Myles Abbott?"

"One moment, please." Everleigh could hear the operator pecking away. "I'm sorry, ma'am, we don't have a patient listed under that name. Is there something else I can help you with?"

"No, thank you."

Getting her purse and sliding into a pair of Nike running shoes, she yelled to her father that she was leaving on her way out the door.

"Ev, hold on!" he called after her. "Where are you going?"

"To check on Myles. I called the hospital, and they said he's not there. He has to be at home."

"Okay. You be careful and let me know what's going on."

"I will."

Everleigh drove fifteen to twenty miles over the speed limit to Myles's house. She was grateful that she didn't get pulled over or in an accident, especially since it was raining. When she arrived, there was an unfamiliar car in his driveway. After parking next to it, she got out so quickly that she almost forgot the keys in the ignition. Using the house key Myles had given her, she let herself in and secured the door behind her.

"Myles," she yelled on her way to his bedroom.

She didn't get a response, but when she stepped inside, her heart sank. Myles was in his bed, propped up with pillows against the headboard, his left arm in a sling, and his legs extended in front of him. A woman was sitting next to him on the outer edge of the bed. When Myles noticed her near the door, he whispered something to the woman, and she turned around. That was when Everleigh recognized her as the woman from the mall.

"What's...going on here?" Everleigh said, barely above a whisper.

"I'm guessin' you here because you heard what happened. Nyema was nice enough to bring me home," Myles answered without looking at Everleigh.

"Oh," she replied before clearing her through. "Thank you, Nyema, you can go now."

"Actually, I—"

"I said, you can go now!" she said a little louder.

"Myles, do you—" Nyema began to protest.

"Look, bitch! If I have to tell you one more time to get the fuck out, I'm gon' beat your ass and drag you out."

"It's cool, Nyema. I'll hit you up if I need anything else."

"No—the fuck—he won't!" Everleigh clarified.

Nyema rose from the bed and slowly walked toward Everleigh, who was still standing by the door. When she walked past her, she rolled her eyes so hard they should have fallen out of her head. Everleigh had something to say, so she followed Nyema to the front door.

"You can lose his number," she told Nyema.

"I didn't call him," she said with a smirk, before walking out.

Everleigh locked the door and marched back to the bedroom. She was pissed that she raced over there, only to find him laid up with another woman. Not to mention, aside from his arm being in a sling, he didn't even look like he'd been hurt, much less, shot.

"Did you call her for a ride?" she asked, surprisingly very calm.

"No. She's a nurse, and she was at the hospital when I got there in the ambulance. When they released me, she was getting off and offered to bring me home, since my truck is still at the shop."

"Bringing you home doesn't mean coming inside and tucking you in. What the fuck was that about, Myles?"

"She insisted."

"So, this is what we're doing?"

"What are you talkin' about, Leigh?" he asked, dismissively.

She approached the bed and sat in the exact spot that Nyema had been sitting. Myles wanted to pull her into his arms, but he was being stubborn and was still in his feelings.

"I hurt you, and now, you want to hurt me. I get it, but there's a difference, Myles."

"How?"

"I knew that me leaving would hurt you, but it was never my intent. In my mind, I was saving your life. You, on the other hand, are using another woman to purposely hurt me. That shit hits different. Now you got that woman thinking she has a chance. If she comes back over here sniffing around your dick, I'm knocking you and her out."

He wanted to laugh at her attempt at being tough, but that probably wouldn't go over well right now. Everleigh was right, though. He knew he had no business letting Nyema come inside, into his bedroom, or onto his bed. He should have just taken the ride and left it at that, but his stubbornness clouded his judgment ...and maybe he was trying to hurt Everleigh a little bit, which was messed up on his part.

"You can think whatever you want, Leigh. I didn't know you were comin' over, so that don't apply here," he told her, not willing to admit she was right.

"Myles, you're almost forty years old and acting twenty. I'm truly sorry that I hurt you. It hurt me to hurt you, but those are decisions I made twelve years ago, as a twenty-two-year-old woman. I took Jory's threats seriously because my gut told me that he was an evil human being. I was terrified of something happening to you and my parents. I thought I was doing the right thing."

The tears that she couldn't shed when she woke up this morning, found their way to her eyelids, and rolled down her cheeks.

"You didn't trust me—"

"It wasn't about trusting you," she shouted, interrupting him. "I knew you would do anything you could to protect me and my parents. But dealing with Jory, the things you would've had to do would've landed you in jail or possibly dead. I didn't want you risking your life or your freedom for me, even if that meant we couldn't be together. Me leaving kept you alive and out of jail, and my parents unharmed. Why can't you understand my position?"

Myles was beginning to break. Everleigh was his weakness and seeing her so upset was making it hard for him to stay angry with her. That was the main reason he told her he needed some time. Being around her would make being angry with her almost impossible, and he wanted to sit in his anger for a little while.

"Nothing woulda happened to me."

"By the grace of God, you managed to avoid prison and death all these years, so I guess I can understand why you may feel like nothing can happen to you. But the truth of the matter is you just don't know. I don't even know what happened last night, but I know enough to know that what that reporter said on the news is nowhere near the truth. Do you know what it felt like when I looked at the TV and saw her standing in front of your shop, saying you'd been shot? You could have easily been the one dead!" she yelled that last part because her emotions got the best of her.

Everleigh shot up from the bed and paced back and forth. Myles could feel the emotion and sincerity behind her words, and she was finally getting through to him.

"Okay, okay. C'mere, baby. Calm down."

He extended his good arm out and motioned for her to come back to the bed.

"No, Myles. I've already suffered some major losses in life. I lost you once, I lost my son, and I just lost my mother. For a minute, I thought maybe God was mending my broken heart when we reunited, but now, I'm not so sure. Don't comfort me and give me a false sense of security if you don't truly want to work things out. Let me go now."

Myles let her words marinate on his brain. Everleigh was his one and only true love, and he knew he wanted to spend the rest of his life with her. Could he look beyond all the things that were revealed to him over the last week and trust that she had nothing else to hide?

"Let you go? That shit will never happen, Leigh."

"Does that mean you forgive me for everything...even agreeing to marry Easton? Because if you're gonna hold it against me and throw the shit in my face when it suits you, you won't have the option to let me go. I'll be already gone."

He extended his arm again, inviting her to come back and sit next to him on the bed. This time, she accepted his invitation.

"Leigh, I can't lie to you. You leavin' me fucked me up. The thought of you lovin' another nigga enough to agree to marry him, fucked me up. Findin' out why you left me created a whole other set of emotions that I can't even explain, but I love you enough to get over that shit, and I love you too much to let you go again."

He paused briefly before continuing.

"While you were gone, almost every night, I dreamed about havin' you again, but I never thought about what that meant. You ain't the same woman that walked out of my life all those years ago. I know that to have you again means I have to truly forgive you, I have to accept all your flaws, and I can't keep holdin' onto the woman that you were when you left, I have to embrace that woman that you are now."

"Are you ready to do those things?"

He looked in her eyes and thought about asking her about Jory's last words to him, but he couldn't bring himself to do it. In his heart of hearts, he knew it wasn't true and that Jory said it to get under his skin. Repeating them to Everleigh would only do more damage to an already fragile situation. So, he took a deep breath and let that shit go.

"I keep tellin' you, you're mine, Leigh. Always have been, always will be."

"So you keep saying."

"It's true. I do have a question, though."

"And what's that?"

"What did you name our son?"

His question caught her off-guard, and she looked down at their joined hands, as she tried to get ahold of her emotions.

"Look at me, baby," he told her.

When she lifted her head, he leaned forward and gently kissed her lips.

"Myles, I never told Jory I was pregnant, he assumed I was, but I didn't know what he would do if he found out. I just wanted to have a healthy pregnancy and give birth to a happy, healthy baby. I never planned to keep him away from you, and the whole time I was pregnant, I called him MJ...Myles Raymond Abbott, Jr. But then..."

Everleigh became too choked up to speak and paused momentarily.

"But then, when he was born, he wasn't breathing. They tried to save him, but..."

"Was there anyone there with you? Your friends?"

"I hadn't met them yet, and I didn't have any other friends."

"Baby, you were all alone?"

"There was this really nice nurse that went above and beyond. She was older, but she helped me a lot. Besides her, I didn't have anyone."

"Damn, baby. That's a lot to carry. I'm sorry about how I handled you and this...situation. You didn't deserve that. I was angry and hurt, but that's no excuse."

"You had a right to react how you reacted. I was wrong, Myles, you don't need to apologize for your reaction."

"So, you named him after me?"

She shook her head. "I couldn't. I started thinking about if you ever had children with someone else, how you might want your son to be named after you."

"Did you really think I'd plant my seeds in another woman?"

She shrugged her shoulders. "Things happen. I named him Raymond Charles Abbott, after you and my dad."

"Do you have pictures?"

She nodded. "I have a whole album and videos documenting my pregnancy. I didn't record the birth because I couldn't do it myself, but I have pictures of him."

"I need to see all of it."

"Okay. It's in a box at my dad's house."

"One more question. How was he...did you...was he cremated or—"

"No, I didn't cremate him."

"I wanna go to his burial site. As soon as we can, I wanna go."

"Okay."

CHAPTER 27

Over the next week, things began to settle down. Myles's shoulder was healing but still sore, and he was no longer using the sling. The police department couldn't find any evidence against Myles in the shooting of Jory, so it was ruled self-defense.

A couple of the guys they used to hustle with pulled up on Myles at his shop, asking a lot of questions. They were more concerned about Jory being connected to them, than the fact that he was dead and that Myles was responsible for it. He didn't feel the need to explain what happened to any of them, but to keep the peace, he told them the same thing he told the police. As long as nothing would be traced back to them, they were cool.

Somehow, he was able to talk his mother and sister from hopping on a plane to check on him. They'd both been FaceTiming him every day, a few times a day since they found out about the shooting. Basically, getting on his last nerve, but he knew it was out of love.

He and Everleigh were in a good place. The morning after the shooting, after they had their heart-to-heart talk, she went home and came back with the box that contained all the pictures and videos documenting her pregnancy. At first, Myles didn't understand why she left him to view it alone, but once he got started, it became clear.

As beautiful as it was to watch, it was just as difficult. The thug in Myles disappeared entirely as he watched a pregnant Everleigh on the screen. It still hurt to know that he wasn't there to experience it with her, but he didn't want to dwell on it. At the end of the video was his son, and he was perfect. He had a head full of curly hair, Myles's chocolate skin, and Everleigh's perfectly shaped lips.

Seeing his son on the video, tore Myles to pieces. He couldn't imagine what state he would have been in, had he been there when his son was born. He thought back to how he treated Everleigh when she told him, and he felt like shit. When she returned, he begged for her forgiveness.

"Baby, I swear, I will never treat you that way again. That was some bitch-nigga shit, and I apologize. I swear, I won't ever treat you like that again. I promise, on our son, you will always be treated like the Queen you are."

They sat on the couch and cried together. It was a cleansing and healing experience for them both. When Everleigh suggested they go to grief therapy, Myles wasn't wholly on board, and it took some convincing. So far, they'd only gone to one session, but it went well, and he planned to continue going.

Now that things were out in the open, Everleigh decided that it was time to tell her best friends about baby Charles. As expected, it was an emotional FaceTime call, but Layne and Robbie didn't judge her and were very supportive. Everleigh felt like sharing her deepest secret, one that she'd been carrying around for over a decade, with the ones she loved, lifted a massive weight from her shoulders. She finally felt free.

"Baby, you almost ready? Daddy already moved our things to your truck, and he's outside waiting," Everleigh called out as she entered Myles's townhome.

"Yeah, my bad. I got caught up on the phone with Tyler. Baby, I'm not so sure about leaving him alone at the shop his first week."

"I understand. That's your baby, and you want to be sure you left it in capable hands. Tyler has more experience doing this than you.

The security cameras have been installed, and you only have one car schedule for each day that we'll be gone. It'll be fine."

"I hope so. I don't wanna have to kill his ass."

"Myles!"

"What? I'm serious. That place is my pride and joy, and if he fuck something up, he gotta go."

Everleigh shook her head, but she knew he was serious. After getting his luggage and securing the house, they piled into his truck and headed for the airport.

THE SHORT FLIGHT WAS OVER RATHER QUICKLY. ONCE THEY picked up the rental car, they were headed to their destination.

"How do you feel?" Myles asked Everleigh.

"I should be asking you and Daddy that. I normally come a few times a year. I visited the last time I was here. You guys good?"

"As good as to be expected, baby girl," her father replied.

Myles couldn't gauge how he felt because his emotions were all over the place. If he had to describe it, he'd say he was nervous and excited.

"I'm good," was all he said in reply.

From LAX to West Los Angeles, it was about a twenty-minute drive. Everleigh pointed out a few sights that they passed along the way. Before long, they had arrived. As they drove through the twists and turns of the path, Myles followed Everleigh's directions until she told him to stop.

"He's over in this area," she told them.

The men exited the vehicle, and Myles went around to help Everleigh out. As they walked around the back of the truck, two Expeditions pulled up and slowed down next to them. Myles reached for his gun but remembered they were in L.A., and he didn't have it. The front and back driver's side window to both trucks slowly went down, revealing who was in each vehicle.

"Wassup, brother-in-law?" Kamden greeted.

Before Myles could respond, car doors were opening, and people appeared out of nowhere. Out of the first truck came Kamden and Jaelynn, with their new baby, and Kyree holding his son. Out of the second truck came Kolby and Myla, with their twins and new baby, along with Myles's mom, Delilah. The only person missing was Braelynn, who was eight months pregnant and probably couldn't travel.

"What the hell are y'all doing here?" Myles asked, still not under-stand what was going on.

"Well, hello to you, too, son." Delilah hugged Myles and kissed him on the cheeks. "We're here because we love you and want you to know you have our support."

"But how did—you know what? I'm not gonna even ask."

Before moving any further, introductions were made, as well as the exchanges of hugs, kisses, handshakes, and daps. Of course, Myla already knew Everleigh and her father. Jaelynn also knew them from her teenage years, although she'd only met Mr. Everette a few times back then.

"I know y'all weren't expecting all of us, so we'll give you some privacy. When you're ready, we'll join you," Delilah said.

Just their presence had both Myles and Everleigh very emotional. Myles nodded and took Everleigh's hand, letting her guide him to the resting place of their firstborn child. When she stopped walking, Myles looked down, and there it was.

"Hey, baby boy. Mommy brought someone very special to meet you today. This is your daddy."

Myles stared at the headstone for a few minutes before speaking.

"Charles Raymond Abbott, held for a moment, loved for a life-time, forever in our hearts," Myles read aloud then looked at Ever-leigh. "That's beautiful, Leigh. Why didn't you tell me his birthday?"

"I don't know. I thought it might be too much with everything else I told you."

Myles squatted down in front of the headstone and put his hand on the top of it.

"It's an honor to share a birthday with you, son. All these years since your mama's been away, I was wonderin' how or why I never got caught up. You've been up there lookin' out for your pops all this time. That's love right there. Even though we could bond like a normal father and son, I love you with everything in me."

When he stood, right away, he wrapped his arms around Everleigh and hugged her so tight, she almost couldn't breathe.

"I love you, Leigh."

"I love you more, Myles."

After a few more minutes alone with their son, they waved the rest of the family over. Myla and Kolby's twins ran ahead of everyone else, both falling but getting right back up. When they reached their uncle, they both wanted to be picked up. He obliged and showered them with kisses. It had been a few months since he'd seen them in person.

Delilah brought her grandson some flowers, so she sat them in front of the headstone, and the rest of the family gathered around for a few moments of silence. Before they made their way back to their vehicles, Myles asked for their attention.

"I'm not sure how y'all ended up here today, I have a feelin' Mr. Everette had a lot to do with it. But regardless, I'm glad you're here."

He got down on one knee in front of Everleigh and pulled out the little black box that he had Mr. Everette retrieve from his luggage. When she realized what was going on, she gasped and put her hand over her mouth.

"Baby, my heart has always belonged to you. Real talk, every day that spent apart, my love for you grew deeper. Most people would probably say this is a long time comin', but I told you, God has a way of workin' things out how they're supposed to be. Right here, right now, in the place where our son was laid to rest, surrounded by our loved ones, and Ms. Dinah and our baby boy smiling down on us, I want you to know that I want to spend the rest of my life with you as my wife. You gon' marry yo' nigga?"

Everyone around them laughed, but Everleigh was on cloud nine.

"Yes, I'm gon' marry my nigga!"

"Good, 'cause that wasn't a question."

Everyone laughed again, including Everleigh, this time. Myles kissed her lips then slid the ring on her finger, happy that it fit. He'd taken it in to get resized, assuming that since her body was a little thicker than it was when he bought the ring, her fingers would be, too, and he was right.

After everyone congratulated the couple, including Braelynn, who Jaelynn had on FaceTime, they finally left the cemetery and headed to the hotel.

CHAPTER 28

After checking into the hotel, they decided to meet for dinner in the hotel restaurant. With sixteen people, including Layne and Robbie, and five of them being children, it was a very lively meal. The only ones that seemed to have a handle on things were Kamden and Jaelynn. Their daughter, Jaeden, was the youngest of the kids, at five months. She was pretty content being breastfed or held by her father.

Kolana, Myla and Kolby's youngest, was a couple weeks older than Jaeden. She was a very calm and mild-mannered baby as well. However, their twins, KJ and Mykha, along with Kyree's son, who they call Ky Junior, as not to be confused with his cousin, were off the chain. When Everleigh and Myles got back to their room, they shared their thoughts on how dinner went.

"Baby, how many kids do you want again?" Everleigh asked.

"Shit, after seein' my nephews and niece together, we might only be able to handle one."

"Oh my God! I was thinking the same thing. Will we have enough energy?"

He laughed. "Well, the good thing about it is we will only have one at a time. From what I know, the twin gene is from the mom's side. Y'all got any twins on your side?"

"Not that I know of, I'll have to ask my dad."

"Cool. You wanna get in the jacuzzi?"

She frowned. "I don't know, baby. You think it's clean?"

Now it was his turn to frown. "As much as this hotel is per night, that muthafucka better be clean."

He marched across into the other room, where the jacuzzi was located. Everleigh shook her head and followed him, but when she entered the room, she stopped in her tracks.

"Oh my God, baby. This is beautiful."

The room with the jacuzzi was adjacent to the bedroom. It was illuminated with lights that look that candles, there were rose petals scattered on the floor and in the jacuzzi, which was filled with water and a small amount of bubbles. There was even jazz music playing softly in the background.

"I'm glad you like it. Do you wanna get in?"

"You think it's safe?"

"Woman, if you don't get naked and get your fine ass in that damn water!"

"Okay, fine! If I catch cooties, I'm blaming you."

"Don't worry, baby. The only thing you gon' catch is my seeds, down your throat, or in them guts. I'll be right back."

"Why are you so damn nasty?" she said to his back.

"'Cause you love that shit," he yelled as he got further away.

When he returned, he was naked, holding a tray of goodies that Everleigh couldn't see because she was seated in the jacuzzi and focused on his semi-hard dick.

"I see something I like."

"You can't even see what's on this tray, baby."

"I'm not talking about what's on that tray."

He looked at her and smirked. "And you say I'm nasty."

After putting the tray on the ledge, he nudged Everleigh to sit up so that he could sit behind her. As she leaned forward, she saw what was on the tray and got excited.

"Chocolate covered strawberries and pineapples? You want that gushy pussy tonight, huh?"

"I want that gushy pussy every night," he told her, before pulling her back into his chest and kissing her neck.

With his long arms, he reached forward and grabbed a strawberry from the tray.

"Open up."

Everleigh leaned her head back and to the side a bit, allowing Myles to feed her.

"Hmm," she moaned at its goodness, causing his dick to bump against her back.

"See, I'm tryin' to relax a lil bit before I dig in them guts. Keep moaning like that, and I'm gon' slide you down on my shit."

"The strawberry is good. I can't express my delight," she said with a giggle.

"Keep it up," he warned.

They sat quietly for a little while, feeding each other and enjoying the jazz music. Now that they were officially engaged, Myles was ready to wedding plans.

"You want a big wedding?" he asked.

"Honestly, it doesn't matter. With my mom being gone, the excitement of planning a big wedding isn't there. I just want to be Mrs. Myles Raymond Abbott."

"Let's do it next week."

"Next week? That's...next week. We don't have time to—"

"Time to what? You said you don't want a big wedding. The only people we need there are my mom and your pops. We can go get the license when we get back and be married by the end of the week."

"Myles, did you already forget how everyone showed up for you today. You don't think they would want to be at your wedding?"

"Baby, I appreciate them for their support, but this ain't about them. It's about me and you. We can record it or go live or whatever it's called. Kyree left Braelynn at home to be here, and she's about ready to pop. Myla will probably be upset, but she'll live. Her and Kolby and those badass kids can stay home."

Everleigh laughed. "You are so wrong for that!"

"Hell, it's true. Kamden and Jaelynn could probably come, but it's unlikely. All of them have businesses to run and families to tend to. I'm not trying to work around none of their schedules. Real talk, if Delilah can't come, I'm good with that, too."

Everleigh thought about for a moment before saying, "Okay, let's do it."

"No shit?"

She leaned back so that she could see his face. Myles was smiling from ear-to-ear.

"I'm ready to be your wife."

Myles gripped her head by the ponytail and pulled, giving him more access to her mouth. Immediately, his tongue was inside, seeking to connect with hers. As their mouths made love, Myles's free hand found his favorite spot between Everleigh's legs. At first, he used the pads of his index and middle finger to massage her clit. She moaned into his mouth and could feel his dick stiffen against her back.

His fingers moved between her lips, and the slickness he felt made his dick throb. When his two fingers found her hole, he slipped them inside, pulling out another moan. He commenced to fucking her with his fingers, now using his thumb on her clit. The pulsing around his fingers that he was searching for began. Everleigh's thighs tightened around his hand as she neared her climax. She pulled her mouth away from his so she could cry out in ecstasy.

"Ahh shit! Baabbyy, I'm cummin'!"

"Give it to me," Myles encouraged.

Seconds later, her fluids were mixing with the bathwater, and Myles didn't give her time to recover. Her pussy was still vibrating when he lifted her up and dropped her on his dick.

"Fuck!" he groaned, with his mouth against her back.

Both of his hands went to fondle her breasts, and she rode his dick. As they fell into a nice rhythm, Myles planted soft kisses all over her back and shoulders.

"Play with that pussy, baby," Myles told her.

Leaning her back against his chest, Everleigh gave him access to her neck while she feverishly rubbed her clit. The combination of his dick pounding her walls, his tongue caressing her neck, and her fingers providing the perfect pressure on her bulging nub, it was long before she was saturating his dick with her slippery juices.

"Damn, baby! You like this dick, huh?"

"I love it!"

Now that she'd reached her peak for the second time, Myles was chasing his nut. His hands went to her side, and he held on tightly pounding relentlessly into her core. Everleigh's hands went to the side of the jacuzzi, as she tried to hold on for the right.

"I'm about to blow! Shit!" he warned, before filling her with his seeds.

Neither of them spoke as they came down from their high. Minutes later, Myles release the stopper, and the water began to drain.

"Turn around, baby," he directed.

She did so, straddling him, then he stood and stepped out of the jacuzzi. Walking them to the bathroom, he turned on the showered and waited for the water to warm up. Everleigh could already feel his dick hardening against her stomach, so she knew they'd go another round or two in the shower.

Not only did they go a few rounds in the shower, when they finally made it to bed, Myles couldn't sleep until he feasted on her center...and that was only the beginning.

CHAPTER 29

"Y'all really didn't have to do all this," Myles told the Ross brothers.

Earlier, when they all met for brunch, Everleigh announced they were getting married the following week. Since everyone wouldn't be able to attend the wedding, they decided to celebrate with a bachelor/bachelorette party at a club while in L.A. Myles invited Droop and his wife, as well. Luckily, Delilah offered to watch all the kids, and Mr. Everette volunteered to help.

"Of course, we did," Kamden said. "We're brothers, and we couldn't let you get married without some kinda celebration."

"Granted, we weren't expecting our wives to tag along, but it's cool," Kolby said, obviously joking.

"First of all, *husband*, I was down for celebrating separately. Layne and Robbie had a nice little strip club in mind for us to go to. Blame your baby brother with his overprotective ass," Myla responded. "We can still—"

"I don't care what y'all say. My wife and the mother of my child was not about to have another man's dick swinging in her face," Kamden interrupted, defending his stance.

"Eww, babe! Not in my face. I don't mind enjoying a sexy male stripper every now and then, but the dick swinging in my face is a no," Jaelynn chimed in.

"You *like* strippers?" Kamden asked, sounding shocked.

"Don't you?" she threw back at him.

"Aye, you two," Myla intervened. "Jae, you know your husband is jealous as hell. Don't get him started."

"You must have forgotten the fit your husband threw when he pulled your ass out of that strip club. Don't be talking about my babe," Jaelynn said in defense of Kamden.

He pulled her into his side and kissed her temple. "That's right, baby. How soon we forget?"

Everyone laughed, including Everleigh, Robbie, and Layne, even though they didn't know the couple very well. Just from the time they'd spent together, they could see how protective Kamden was of his wife.

"First of all," Robbie said, raising her hand to get everyone's attention. "Where the hell in Chicago did y'all find these niggas?"

"Right," Layne added. "And is it only three of y'all?"

The group laughed again, but Robbie and Layne were serious.

"We didn't even meet them in Chicago. It all started with my sister Braelynn and Kyree. I'll tell you the story before we leave L.A.," Jaelynn promised.

"We gon' hold you to it. You would think, living in or this close to L.A., there would be an abundance of fine ass men. However, it looks like we need to move to Seattle or Chicago, 'cause ain't nothin' here," Layne said.

"Hell, yeah!" Robbie added. "These niggas got y'all glowing and shit while we sitting around in the Golden State, looking dry and thirsty."

Robbie's comment got another round of laughter. The rest of the night was more of the same. The drinks flowed, although Myla and Jaelynn couldn't indulge because they were still nursing. A few times, the ladies left the VIP area and went down to the dance floor. Of course, they were dressed to kill, and all eyes were on them.

As the guys watched them from above, they heard the beat of a family song. Kyree, Kolby, and Kamden had a flashback to a few years ago when they were in Belize with the girls. Giving each other a knowing look, they looked at the dancefloor and shook their heads.

"Damn, I'm glad Braelynn ain't here," came from Kyree.

"They're about to do that damn routine," Kamden said.

After handing their drinks to their brother, Kamden and Kolby raced down the stairs, two at a time. Pushing through the crowd, they made it to the dancefloor as a small group gathered around Jaelynn and Myla. Just like in Belize, they got to them just before they were about to drop into a split.

"I swear to God, Jae!"

"What the fuck, baby!"

Kamden and Kolby both shouted over the music, as they wrapped their arms around the waists of their wives and carried them off the dancefloor. Jaelynn and Myla didn't even put up a fight. They knew as soon as they heard the beat drop to "Tambourine" by Eve and started doing the dance routine they made when they were in their teens, that their husbands would be there in a matter of minutes. All the other ladies followed them back up to VIP. As soon as the ladies sat down, their husbands began to fuss.

"I can't believe we're doing this shit again," Kamden complained.

"Again? You weren't successful the first time, remember," Jaelynn reminded.

"My, you got three kids. Were you really out there about to do the splits in the middle of the dancefloor?" Kolby asked, sounding pissed.

"You should be happy that your wife still got it like that," Myla said before kissing his lips.

The first time the guys saw them doing the same routine in Belize, Braelynn was with them. Their reaction was the same back then, too.

"One of these days, y'all gon' let us get through our whole damn routine," Jaelynn griped.

"Baby, if you wanna do that routine for *me* when we get back to the hotel, I'll put the damn song on repeat, and you can do your thang. But all that ass shaking, air grinding, and splits is too much in front of all these people."

"Real shit!" Kolby agreed as he and his brother connected their fists.

"Y'all wild as hell," Myles said, laughing at the couples.

"Are y'all always like this?" Everleigh asked.

"Like what?" Kamden said as if their behavior was perfectly normal.

"This is them, baby. Now you know what to expect when we go to Chicago," Myles assured her.

"Don't forget about us when y'all go to Chicago," Layne chimed in.

"Yeah, I'm sure y'all got some cousins or something for us," Robbie added.

The rest of the night was more of the same, but instead of going to the dancefloor, the ladies shook their asses in VIP. After leaving the club, they went to breakfast, and by the time they made it back to the hotel, it was close to four in the morning.

After sexing Myles all night their first night in town, then partying until the wee hours of the morning and sexing a little more when they got back to the hotel, she was tempted to cancel the photoshoots that she had scheduled the later that morning and afternoon. She'd also told Myles to bring the family to the studio later that day because she thought it would be adorable to take some pictures of all the kids. Instead of cuddling up next Myles, she rolled out of bed and started the day.

After buying the largest cup of coffee available, she put on a pair of sunglasses and made her way to the studio. Once she got started, things flowed well. The first shoot was of a young couple who'd recently gotten engaged. The young lady was the daughter of a well-known rapper that Everleigh had worked with a while back. He'd hired her for many different occasions and refused to let anyone else take his daughter's engagement photos.

The second shoot was maternity photos. The couple was having their first child together, but the father already had a five-year-old son that they included in the shoot as well. Both shoots went well, and Everleigh was excited to edit them, which is what she did for the next couple of hours.

Her eyes were beginning to cross, but thankfully, she was almost done. She'd forgotten that the whole crew would be coming to take pictures until the buzzer requesting entrance to her studio sounded. After confirming that it was them, she pressed the button to allow entry, saved what she was working on, and left her office to greet everyone.

"I was so wrapped up in my editing, I forgot y'all were coming," she said before standing on her toes and kissing her fiancé.

Kolby and Myla were both holding one of the twins, and as soon as they put them down, they took off in the same direction.

"My, get your badass kids," Myles complained to his sister.

"Aye, bruh, don't be talking about my seeds like that. They're not bad, there's just two of them, and they do everything together, which makes them seem worse," Kolby reasoned.

"Naw, bruh, those two are bad, and y'all need to get it under control before you can't," Kyree added, holding Ky Jr. in his arms.

"KJ and Mykha, leave that alone," Myla yelled as she headed in their way.

"It's okay, Myla. Those are the toys I use when I have kids come for shoots. They can play with them," Everleigh told her.

"You sure you still wanna do this? We can find something to do while you finish," Myles offered.

"No, it's fine. I was almost done. Where's Ms. Delilah and my dad?" She noticed they were missing once she'd greeted everyone.

He laughed a hearty laugh. "Your dad is probably still sleeping. The kids wore him *out* last night. My mom, Ms. Social Butterfly herself, met up with one of her friends from high school. She said she let us have our fun last night and not to wait up for her."

"Oh, well damn. Is this a male or female friend?"

"Don't play with me, Leigh. I hadn't even thought of that. It better not be no nigga."

"Baby, Ms. Delilah is extra grown. You better stay outta her business," she teased. "Let me go get my stuff, and we can get started. When we're done, we can get something to eat and take the kids to a park afterward. The twins can play and burn off some more energy."

"I know you lowkey talking about my babies, Ev. It's cool,

though. I can't wait until y'all have some babies, and they run y'all ragged," Myla teased.

"I'm a couple years older than you and starting a little later. Why would you wish that on me?"

About an hour and a half later, the kids and the adults were getting cranky, but Everleigh got some excellent shots.

"I swear you have the patience of Job," Jaelynn said. "I would have given up when the first kid started crying."

"Me too," Myla added. "How often do you do shoots with kids?"

"Not very often, but when I do, it's newborns or older kids," Everleigh replied.

"Braelynn is gonna be pissed," Kyree said.

The shoot started off with just the kids, but somehow, the whole Ross family ended up in it. Braelynn is definitely going to be upset.

"She sure is, and I'm glad I don't have to answer to her," Kolby commented, not helping the situation.

"If she's upset, tell her that I promise to come to Chicago and do a whole shoot after she has the baby," Everleigh offered.

"Oh, that will soften the blow, so I'm gonna hold you to that promise," Kyree said.

After locking up the studio, they went to dinner, then to a park, where they were successful with tiring out the twins. Once they got back to the hotel, they went their separate ways, promising to see each other for brunch before catching their flights back home. It wasn't the trip that Everleigh and Myles had planned, but it was exactly what they needed.

CHAPTER 30

The morning of Myles and Everleigh's wedding day had arrived. The night before, she stayed at her father's house, and he would be driving her to the courthouse when it was time. She woke up early, with her mother heavy on her mind, and a little sad that she wouldn't physically be there. It had been almost four months since she died, but so much had happened in such a short amount of time, it seemed like much more time had passed.

Getting out of bed, she washed her face and brushed her teeth before pulling on a hoodie and a pair of sweats. Just in case her father woke up before she returned, she left him a note on the refrigerator. About twenty-five minutes later, she was pulling into the cemetery where her mother was buried. With everything going on, this was the first time she'd been back since the burial, although her father came once a week.

The grass was wet, so she grabbed a blanket from the backseat. Once she found her mother's headstone, she placed the blanket in front of it and took a seat. For about ten minutes, she sat quietly, feeling her mother's spirit around her. Then the tears started, and for another ten minutes, she allowed herself to release them freely. Finally, she was able to talk.

"Ma, I miss you so much. People always say that your parents can't be your best friend, but that's not true. You were my best friend. I bet you're probably saying, *'Well, if I was your best friend, why didn't you tell me why you left and about my grandson?'* I was scared, Ma, and I wanted to protect you, Daddy, and Myles. That's all it boils down to...my fear and my desire to protect.

I planned to tell you about baby Charles after I had him, but when he died, I thought it might be better if nobody knew. That was a painful experience, Ma, even more painful than losing you, to be honest. I didn't want the people that I loved, especially Myles, to feel the hurt that I felt after losing my baby."

"Leigh," she heard behind her, causing her to jump.

"Oh shit, Myles. You scared—what are you doing here?"

"I don't know. Woke up, and this is where I was led to be."

She moved over and made room for him on the blanket. He sat next to her and put his arm around her shoulders.

"You good?"

"I am."

"I wasn't tryin' to eavesdrop, but I heard what you said to your mom. Baby, I forgave you, your pops forgave you, and if Ms. Dinah was here, she would, too. Don't hold on to that shit no more. My bad, Ms. Dinah."

"I know, baby. I just felt the need to talk to her about it. If you want, I can leave you alone. I'm sure you weren't expecting me to be here," she offered.

"I wasn't, but I don't mind talkin' in front of you."

"Okay."

"Ms. Dinah, I finally got my girl. The only thing missin' from this is you. I know you here in spirit, but this day would be perfect if you were here physically. I wanted to bring her here to propose, but when I found out about our son, I had a change of plans. I hope that's cool."

He looked at Everleigh when he felt her gaze on him.

"Why you staring?" he asked.

"How long have you been planning to propose?"

"The first time or this time."

"There was more than one time?"

"I bought your engagement ring before you moved to L.A. Leigh, I was days away from doing exactly what you'd been asking me to do. I had one more shipment, and that was it. I was gon' propose to you a couple days later."

Knowing how close Myles was to leaving the streets and proposing to her, and thinking about how she left him, broke her heart.

"Oh my God, Myles. Baby, I'm so sorry. The way I left you was so...how could you take me back so easily after I broke your heart."

"Remember when I told you that everything happens when it's supposed to happen." She nodded. "Had we crossed paths ten years ago, eight years ago, five years ago, hell, maybe even a year ago, I don't know if I would have taken you back so easily. It took me a long to get over you leaving."

"But you kept the ring all this time."

"I did. What else was I gon' do with it? It woulda been messed up to give it to someone else, not that I was even thinking about doing that. As hurt as I was, there was always a part of me that was waiting for you. Something inside told me that we'd be together again."

"What about this time? How long were you planning it?"

"Probably the moment I laid eyes on you at the hospital."

"Really?"

"Yep."

They sat and talked for a while longer, to each other and Ms. Dinah. Before they parted ways, Everleigh realized something.

"Baby, it's our wedding day. We aren't supposed to see each other."

"Woman, we've had all the bad luck we gon' get. I ain't claiming that shit." He kissed her lips and opened her car door. "Now, I'll see your sexy ass at the courthouse."

HOURS LATER, EVERLEIGH AND HER FATHER PARKED AT THE courthouse. He turned the car off and looked at her.

"You ready?"

"I'm more than ready, Daddy."

"Myles has always been like a son to me. I'm happy that you found your way back to each other, and I'm sure your mother is smiling in heaven."

"I hope so. We had a good talk this morning. In my rush to get ready, I forgot to tell you that Myles showed up there as well."

Everette smiled because hearing that brought him great joy.

"You know what they say, great minds think alike. Sounds like you two were on the same page this morning. Now let's go get you married."

Everleigh waited for her father to come around and open her door. After helping her out, they held hands and walked to the courthouse entrance. Once they got through security, she wanted to check her makeup.

"Daddy, I'm gonna go to the bathroom. Wait for me here."

She stepped inside the bathroom and went to the full-length mirror. Looking at herself in the reflection, she admired her beauty. All of her curls were pulled into a tight bun on the top of her head, with her baby hairs laid to perfection, and two little curls just below each temple.

The dress she chose was white, with an A-line cut and one shoulder sweep. The material was chiffon, and the front split went all the way up to her hip. Her shoes were four-inch, open-toed, stiletto heels, covered in rhinestones, that matched the tiara that she removed from her purse and placed carefully on her head. Just because she was getting married at the courthouse didn't mean she couldn't be sexy and feel like a princess. Back in the hallway, her father smiled when she reappeared.

"You'll always be my princess," he said, kissing her forehead.

They held hands again and walked to their destination. As they neared the corner that they were to go around, Everleigh heard a bunch of voices. Her heart sank a bit because she was hoping that there wouldn't be a lot of people getting married along with them. When they rounded the corner, the group that the voices belong to yelled, "Surprise!" and she almost broke down.

Looking around, she saw everyone that was in L.A. last week, including her best friends, Robbie and Layne. She couldn't believe her eyes, and her heart was filled with so much joy.

"Oh my God! I can't believe you're all here."

"I'm here, too," Everleigh heard but didn't see the owner of the voice.

Kyree held up his phone and turned it toward her. It was Brae-lynn, pregnant as ever, on the screen.

"We wouldn't have missed this for the world," Myla said.

"Wow! This is unbelievable," Everleigh exclaimed. "I know coming here after being in L.A. just last week was a lot. This means so much."

Her eyes searched the group, looking for Myles, but she didn't see him. Suddenly, the small group began to separate, leaving a small aisle for her to walk through, and there he was, standing on the other end, looking fine as ever. As her eyes roamed his body, her heart skipped a beat. The only other time she'd ever seen him slightly dressed up was for her mother's funeral, and for that, he was much more casual.

For his wedding day, Myles stepped out of his comfort zone. He wore black dress pants, with a black and white paisley print shirt, untucked, and the top two buttons open. To finish off his look, he wore diamond studs in both ears, a black suit jacket, and a pair of black Ferragamo signature loafers. When Everleigh noticed his shoes, she was shocked because she'd never seen him in anything but Jordans.

"Bring your fine ass on so we can get married," he commanded.

She didn't realize that she was still holding her father's hand until she released it. When she made it to Myles, he wrapped his arms around her waist, lifted her in the air, and spun her around as they kissed.

"I love you," he told her when their mouths disconnected.

"I love you more."

"Come on and marry yo' nigga then, baby."

EPILOGUE

Three Years Later

"Ev, it'll be fine. You need to calm down," Myla told her sister-in-law.

"The hell it will! My, I can't keep having all these kids. My ass is tired, and I'm too old for this shit."

Myles and Everleigh were visiting Chicago for a few days, with their two children, two-year-old son, Myles Jr., and one-year-old daughter, MyLeigh Dinah. Everleigh hadn't been feeling well, and Myla was trying to convince her to take a pregnancy test.

"Seriously, Ev, what's one more? You already have two. I have a test downstairs," Myla offered.

Myla and Kolby had recently purchased a bigger home because, with four kids, they'd run out of room in their first home.

"Damn, My," Braelynn said. "Kolby still got you thinking you're pregnant every month?"

"Y'all, the man is crazy. I told him after I had Kolman that I was done and getting my tubes tied. Do y'all know the nigga cried? I can't deal with his ass. We got four kids, all under the age of five, and he don't wanna use protection. What is wrong with him?"

"Brae, I know you're not talking. Your ass is pregnant with number three right now," Jaelynn reminded her. "Y'all aren't too far behind them."

"True! Let me shut my ass up. Those tests that Myla got stored under the sink come in handy as hell."

Braelynn discovered she was pregnant all three times with one of Myla's many tests.

"Jaelynn, you're the only one that seems to have some kind of control. How the hell are you only on baby number two?" Everleigh asked.

"Because Kamden wants four to six kids and I told him that if I agreed to have that many kids, they had to be spaced apart. I can't do that back-to-back shit. I need my sanity," she told them as she nursed her six-month-old son Kamden Jr.

"And he agreed? What do y'all use for birth control?" Myla asked.

"He uses condoms."

"What?" Everleigh, Braelynn, and Myla all said simultaneously.

"How do you get him to do that?" Everleigh asked.

"If he wants some pussy, he doesn't have a choice. Plain and simple. Y'all better learn how to put your foot down or, better yet, close your legs until they listen. In their eyes, pussy in a condom-covered dick is better than no pussy at all."

The three other ladies sat in silence, processing Jaelynn's words like she had just told them the cure for cancer.

"Give me the damn test, My. If it's positive, I'm done after this. I'll be applying some of Jaelynn's rules around my damn house," Everleigh decided.

The three of them went to the basement, walking past their husband and kids, to the extra bedroom. Myla retrieved one of the many pregnancy tests from under the sink and handed it to Everleigh.

"Good luck, sis," she told her, leaving her in the bathroom.

Everleigh closed the door and prepared to pee on the stick.

Before she could finish, there was a knock on the door. Myles had entered without waiting for her to reply.

"Baby, the kids will be occupied for the next ten, maybe fifteen minutes. Let me get some pussy right quick." Then he noticed what she was doing. "Is that a pregnancy test?"

"Yes."

"You think you pregnant?" he asked, eyes filled with excitement.

"I am."

It had barely been a minute, and the test was already showing a positive result. She showed it to Myles before wrapping it in some toilet paper and sitting it on the counter, then washing her hands. He wrapped his arms around her from behind, squeezing her tight, then resting his hands on her flat stomach.

"My baby givin' me another baby," he mumbled into her neck, but Everleigh could still hear the emotion in his voice.

When he lifted his head, their eyes met in the mirror above the sink. In his, she saw pure joy, happiness, and love.

Before she took the pregnancy test, the possibility of being pregnant with their third child in three years seemed daunting. Now, those temporary feelings seemed foolish, and she felt terrible for thinking that way.

"What's wrong, baby?" Myles asked when her eyes filled with tears. He put his hands on her shoulders and turned her around to face him.

She shook her head as she wiped the tears from her eyes. "Nothing, baby. I'm really happy, and I love you so much."

"I love you more."

A few years ago, Myles could only dream moments like the one they were having. To be holding Everleigh in his arms, as his wife, his lover, and his best friend, knowing that she was carrying their fourth child together, made his life complete. Love isn't always easy, but to have her again made every struggle worth it.

THE END

AFTERWORD

Dear Readers,

When I tell you Myles did not have a story, he did not have a story. His character was strictly there to be the overprotective big brother. However, when almost every review asked about him, I had to tell his story. I hope you all enjoyed it. Thank you all for encouraging me to strive to reach the next level. If you could please leave a review on Amazon and/or Goodreads, I would greatly appreciate it. Until next time.

Kay Shanee

LET'S CONNECT!

You can find me at all of the following:

Reading Group: Kay Shanee's Reading Korner – After Dark
Facebook page: Author Kay Shanee
Instagram: @AuthorKayShanee
Goodreads: Kay Shanee
Subscribe to my mailing list: Subscribe to Kay Shanee
Website at www.AuthorKayShanee.com

OTHER BOOKS BY KAY SHANEE

Love Hate and Everything in Between

Love Doesn't Hurt

Love Unconventional

I'd Rather Be With You

Can't Resist This Complicated Love

Love's Sweet Serenade

The Love I Deserve

Loving Him Through The Storm

Since the Day We Met

Easy to Love

Heal My Heart

COMPLETED SERIES

Until the Wheels Fall Off

Until the Wheels Fall Off...Again

Could This Be Love - Part 1

Could This Be Love -Part 2

CPSIA information can be obtained
at www.ICGtesting.com
Printed in the USA
LVHW081753061120
670969LV00012B/1516